PENGUIN BOOKS

MAURICE, OR THE FISHER'S COT

Mary Shelley was born in 1797, the only daughter of William Godwin and Mary Wollstonecraft. In 1814 she eloped abroad with Percy Bysshe Shelley; they finally settled in Italy in 1818. After Shelley's death in 1822 she returned to England and lived on till 1851. Her most famous work is *Frankenstein*, which was published in 1818.

Claire Tomalin was born in London in 1933. She became literary editor first of the *New Statesman* and then of the *Sunday Times*. She is the author of *The Life and Death of Mary Wollstonecraft*, which won the Whitbread First Book Prize for 1974; *Shelley and His World* (reissued by Penguin in 1992); *Katherine Mansfield: A Secret Life* (Penguin 1988), *The Invisible Woman: The Story of Nelly Ternan and Charles Dickens* (Penguin 1991), which won the NCR Book Award for 1991, as well as the Hawthornden Prize and the 1990 James Tait Black Memorial Prize for Biography: *Mrs Jordan's Profession* (Penguin 1995); and the highly acclaimed *Jane Austen: A Life* (Penguin 1998).

D0334155

MARY SHELLEY

Maurice, or the Fisher's Cot

Edited with an Introduction
by Claire Tomalin

PENGUIN BOOKS

PENGUIN BOOKS

Published by the Penguin Group
Penguin Books Ltd, 27 Wrights Lane, London w8 5tz, England
Penguin Putnam Inc., 375 Hudson Street, New York, New York 10014, USA
Penguin Books Australia Ltd, Ringwood, Victoria, Australia
Penguin Books Canada Ltd, 10 Alcorn Avenue, Toronto, Ontario, Canada m4v 3b2
Penguin Books (NZ) Ltd, Private Bag 102902, NSMC, Auckland, New Zealand

Penguin Books Ltd, Registered Offices: Harmondsworth, Middlesex, England

First published by Viking 1998
Published in Penguin Books 1999
1 3 5 7 9 10 8 6 4 2

The acknowledgements on pp. xi–xii constitute an extension of this copyright page

The moral right of the author of the introduction has been asserted

Set in Monotype Baskerville
Printed in England by Clays Ltd, St Ives plc

CONTENTS

List of Illustrations vii

Acknowledgements xi

Preface by Cristina Dazzi xiii

Introduction by Claire Tomalin 1

Note on the Text 55

Maurice, or the Fisher's Cot 57

Maurice: Showing the Author's Original
　　Lineation, Pagination, Spelling, Corrections
　　and Emendations 89

Appendix: 'Twelve Cogent Reasons for
　　Supposing P.B. Sh–ll–y to be the D–v–l
　　Inc–rn–t–' by Lady Mountcashell 137

Notes 143

Bibliographical Note 151

The Family Tree of Mary Shelley 154

The Family Tree of Lady Mountcashell 156

LIST OF ILLUSTRATIONS

(between pp. 32-33)

Mary Wollstonecraft, engraving by J. Chapman after an unknown artist, published 1798 (private collection)

Lady Mountcashell, from a miniature attributed to Charles Robertson (1759-1821) (Cini archive, San Marcello Pistoiese)

Posthumous portrait of Mary Shelley by Reginald Easton (1807-93) (Bodleian Library, Oxford)

Laurette Tighe, *c.* 1830, from a drawing by an unknown artist (The Carl H. Pforzheimer Collection of *Shelley and His Circle*, The New York Public Library. Astor, Lenox and Tilden Foundations)

William Godwin, 1802, oil on canvas by James Northcote (National Portrait Gallery, London)

Percy Bysshe Shelley, 1819, oil on canvas by Amelia Curran (National Portrait Gallery, London)

Claire Clairmont, 1819, oil on canvas by Amelia Curran (City of Nottingham Museums, Newstead Abbey)

Lord Byron, *c.* 1818, engraving after G. H. Harlow (John Murray Collection)

William Shelley, Rome, 1819, oil on canvas by Amelia Curran (The Carl H. Pforzheimer Collection of *Shelley and His Circle*, The New York Public Library. Astor, Lenox and Tilden Foundations)

Allegra, Venice, 1818, unknown artist (John Murray Collection)

Lady Mountcashell, from a physionotrace engraving made in Paris by Edme Queneday (1756-1830) (The Carl H. Pforzheimer Collection of *Shelley and His Circle*, The New York Public Library. Astor, Lenox and Tilden Foundations)

Pisa, engraving by C. Heath after a drawing by E. F. Batty, published 1818 (Hulton Getty)

Nerina Tighe, *c.* 1830, from a drawing by an unknown artist (The Carl H. Pforzheimer Collection of *Shelley and His Circle*, The New York Public Library. Astor, Lenox and Tilden Foundations)

Laurette, late 1840s, photograph (Cini archive, San Marcello Pistoiese)

Placido Tardy, late 1840s, photograph (Cini archive, San Marcello Pistoiese)

Laurette, *c.* 1870, photograph (Cini archive, San Marcello Pistoiese)

Placido Tardy, *c.* 1870, photograph (Cini archive, San Marcello Pistoiese)

Lady Mountcashell, 1835, watercolour, by Diana King (courtesy of Col. A. L. King-Harman)

(between pp. 112–113)

Maurice, Part I, page 1 of the original manuscript (Cini archive, San Marcello Pistoiese)

Part III, page 24 of the original manuscript (Cini archive, San Marcello Pistoiese)

Torquay, Devon, early nineteenth-century engraving, artist unknown (Hulton Getty)

Eton, *c.* 1830–40, engraving by William Evans of Eton (Hulton Getty)

Ilfracombe, Devon, early nineteenth-century engraving, artist unknown (Hulton Getty)

Page 19 of the original manuscript (Cini archive, San Marcello Pistoiese)

Page 20 of the original manuscript (Cini archive, San Marcello Pistoiese)

Page 38 of the original manuscript (Cini archive, San Marcello Pistoiese)

LIST OF ILLUSTRATIONS

Page 39 of the original manuscript (Cini archive, San Marcello Pistoiese)

Mary Shelley, exhibited 1840, oil on canvas by Richard Rothwell (National Portrait Gallery, London)

Endpapers: Livorno, coloured engraving by Giuseppe Maria Terreni (1739–1811) in Biblioteca Nazionale, Florence (Scala)

Frontispiece: Maurice, Part I, page 1 of the original manuscript (Cini archive, San Marcello Pistoiese)

ACKNOWLEDGEMENTS

My first thanks are to Cristina and Andrea Dazzi and to Signora Giovanna Dazzi, née Farina Cini, for so generously sharing their discovery with me; for allowing me to use and quote from their archives; for all the work they have put into searching for information; and for their many kindnesses, their hospitality and their friendship. Cristina Dazzi especially has been tireless in working on the details of this book.

Nora Crook, General Editor of *Novels and Selected Works of Mary Shelley* and Reader in English at Anglia Polytechnic University, Cambridge, has given me support, encouragement and invaluable advice.

Catherine Payling, Curator of the Keats–Shelley Museum in Rome, has also done a great deal to help at all stages.

Col. A. L. King-Harman gave me valuable information, lent me books, led me to Lady Mountcashell's letters in Brian MacDermot's book, and allowed his portrait of Lady Mountcashell to be photographed for this book.

William St Clair generously allowed me to inspect his collection of books, in particular early nineteenth-century children's books.

I am grateful also to Dr Bruce Barker-Benfield of the Bodleian Library; to Lord Abinger; to Louis Amigues,

Directeur des Archives et de la Documentation at the Quai d'Orsay; to Daniele Danesi of the Biblioteca Comunale Forteguerriana at Pistoia; to Laura Desideri; to Deborah Jeffs; to Peter Stothard, Editor of *The Times*, and to Richard Owen, the paper's Rome correspondent; and to Harriet Cullen, Chairman of the Keats–Shelley Memorial Association.

The British Library, the London Library, the Bodleian and the Gabinetto Vieusseux in Florence have all been of great assistance.

I should also like to acknowledge generous help from the British Council in Italy and British Airways in Italy.

At Viking Penguin I have once again had the benefit of Tony Lacey's editorial advice and Donna Poppy's meticulous attention to the text, this being the fifth book on which we three have very happily worked together. Gráinne Kelly's picture research has been another essential part of the process; and Valentina Rice helped us with some translation.

I have been particularly pleased to be involved with a project that brings together several European countries, Italy, Ireland, England and France, and demonstrates the strength and continuity of our links.

PREFACE

The story that you are about to read was found at the beginning of the summer of 1997.

A few pages written with an orderly handwriting, tied in two thin bindings with a pale blue cover, which did little to please the eye. They were mixed up with a pile of personal letters, school diplomas, poems and dedications, economic and political pamphlets, newspaper cuttings, visiting cards, train tickets, maps and photographs. A bit of everything.

Simply because there was a bit of everything, I went to rummage through that box in the library. I hoped I might find something interesting to be able to take to an exhibition in Pisa in November. An exhibition about the winter of 1827/8 in Pisa, when the poet Leopardi visited the city and met Mrs Mason and her daughter Laurette.

I took the box and started selecting documents, looking only at the dates and to whom they referred, and I found nothing except for the odd letter from husband to wife regarding the rearing of the children, Laurette and Nerina (Nerina, a few years later, became our great-great-grandmother).

Suddenly, I found this little book in my hands and I read the dedication at the top of the first page: 'To Laurette from her friend Mrs Shelley'. I thought I had misread it and went back to the house in order to be able to transcribe it at my leisure. I knew that the Shelleys had been in Pisa and had seen Mrs Mason and her children, but I never thought that there had been so much affection and intimacy between them!

I'm not an expert on Mary Shelley, and like many of you have read only *Frankenstein*. I was not aware of everything she had published and merely thought it could be one of the many things of hers that I had not heard of.

And so, little by little, I began doing some research and I came to realize that it could really be hers and previously unpublished, but for months I had no confirmation.

Then, the Keats–Shelley Museum of Rome gave me the addresses of two specialists and I wrote to them.

Splendid! I received confirmation that all was true. The pages that I touched and retouched, to read and transcribe what I could of the nineteenth-century handwriting, were chosen with love by the famous Mary for a child who was my aunt.

Cristina Dazzi
San Marcello Pistoiese, 1998

INTRODUCTION

I

Returning from a week's holiday in early November 1997, I found in the long loop of faxes delivered during my absence one from Italy. It was handwritten, and the signature at the end meant nothing to me: Cristina Dazzi. She told me she had come upon what she thought was a 'novel autograph unpublished by Mary Shelley'. She gave its title, 'Maurice, or the Fisher's Cot'; and, although her English was not quite perfect, I had no trouble understanding her description of the 'little book of a few pages, sewed with a string and covered by a thicker paper, inside the cover the words "alla Signora Shelley", perhaps it was a paper bundle piece which Mary used to sew the little leaves, and at the top of the first page: "For Laurette from her friend Mrs Shelley".' Signora Dazzi went on to say that her husband's family had been close to the Shelleys in the 1820s; and she asked for my advice.

An unpublished story by Mary Shelley would be an exciting discovery; but a children's story? I knew of none by her. I telephoned Nora Crook, a friend and a fine Shelley scholar, and we talked the subject over. Mary Shelley's Italian journal records that she did write a story 'for Laurette' on 10 August 1820. There is also a letter from Mary's father, William Godwin, who ran a publishing firm specializing in works for children (the Juvenile Library), telling her that a story called *Maurice* which she has sent him is too short for publication. His letter is dated 10 October 1821, and nothing more was heard of the story until 1976, when the American scholar Charles E. Robinson published an edition of Mary Shelley's short stories, and conjectured that the 'story for Laurette' and the lost 'Maurice', 'never located', were one and the same. It looked as if he could be right.[1]

I faxed all these snippets of information to Cristina Dazzi, for whom they were new and welcome. And I went on exploring the background, and thinking about Mary Shelley: the more I read, the better the provenance looked. The Laurette for whom the story was originally written was the daughter of two Irish friends of the Shelleys living in Pisa, George Tighe and Margaret, Lady Mountcashell, then known as 'Mrs Mason'; and Laurette's younger sister, Nerina, was Signor Dazzi's great-great-grandmother. Cristina Dazzi and I exchanged further faxes, and I decided I ought to go to Italy.

I got out a map to find San Marcello Pistoiese, where the Dazzis live. It is a small Tuscan town in the Apennine hills above Pistoia. Then I rang the editor of *The Times*, Peter Stothard, who takes an interest in literary stories. He offered to send me to Italy if I would write about this one, and if I would go there before other papers in England or America were on to it. I agreed, gratefully. His foreign desk booked me on to an immediate flight to Florence, and arranged for their correspondent in Rome, Richard Owen, to drive to San Marcello, bringing with him Catherine Payling of the Keats–Shelley Museum to meet me there.

I set off for Gatwick at once, with my husband's farewell warning in my ears: 'Remember the Hitler diaries.' Fortunately Mary Shelley's handwriting is easier to recognize, and to decipher, than Hitler's *Deutsche Schrift*. Still, it felt like an adventure: certainly a change from a day at the British Library. The plane was delayed, the weather menacing, and I arrived in the dark at Florence Airport to find no taxis. When at last I managed to summon one we sped along the motorway and then up into the hills. Sleet was falling, the road was slippery and rose in sharp bends. At moments I could see lights gleaming on the plain below, then they were lost. There was fog about too. When we reached San Marcello, the driver had to ask for the hotel, Il Cacciatore – 'The Hunter'. It was on the road out of town, one of those boxlike modern buildings, but the people were friendly, and Richard and Catherine had just arrived. We ate our pasta together, followed by a dish of local chestnuts – the hillsides are covered with chestnut woods – and we wondered what was in store for us the next day.

II

Mary Shelley has interested me since the 1970s, when I researched my first book, *The Life and Death of Mary Wollstonecraft*, which was about her mother. I followed it with a study of Shelley; this time Mary Shelley was a central figure. After this I kept up with whatever was published relating to her, and in 1997 I was a curator for a bicentenary exhibition celebrating mother and daughter. One way and another, I have lived with the family for twenty-five years. They have never lost their fascination for me, and I have seen Mary Shelley emerge slowly from the overshadowing reputation of her poet husband to take her place as one of the key figures of the Romantic movement. There have been several biographies. Her tales and stories were published in 1976, her journals in 1987. Many hitherto unknown letters of hers have been tracked down and published in Betty T. Bennett's fine three-volume edition between 1980 and 1988; and in 1996 all her novels were republished in eight volumes. Her step-sister Claire Clairmont's journals and letters have been published too – in 1968 and 1995 respectively – adding to our knowledge of Mary; and the ongoing publication of volumes in the Carl H. Pforzheimer Library's *Shelley and His Circle* continues to make more manuscript material available.

If there is now almost a Mary Shelley industry, she is still best known for her novel *Frankenstein*. *Frankenstein* was an extraordinary achievement for a twenty-year-old, with its blend of horror, philosophy and scientific speculation: an account of a man who revivifies dead men's bones to make a living creature, and then repents his experiment when he finds he has produced a monster with a will of his own. She went on to write other less disturbing novels;

but *The Last Man* (1826) was another grim fantasy, in which
the human race is wiped out by epidemic disease.

If monsters and the annihilation of the human race are
surprising subjects for a young wife and mother, they seem
less so when you look at the detail of her life. Mary Shelley
was the child of two outstanding parents, the philosopher
and novelist William Godwin, and Mary Wollstonecraft,
famous for her pioneering statement of women's rights,
and also a novelist; but the birth of the younger Mary
killed her mother. This was in 1797. Godwin was left
grieving to care for her and her three-year-old half-sister
Fanny. The children grew up with the portrait of their
dead mother looking down from the wall. They were not
best pleased when a stepmother, Mrs Clairmont, joined
the household, bringing a son and daughter of her own,
and there were always tensions within the family. There
were also wider problems caused by the backlash against
radical ideas, which meant that Mary Wollstonecraft and
William Godwin were both more derided than admired
as their daughter was growing up.

Godwin was a good father. He expected much of his
children, and they enjoyed rare privileges. They had the
run of his library, and met his many visitors, among them
Coleridge, who read his *Ancient Mariner* aloud as they
listened from behind the sofa. Godwin realized early that
Mary was greatly gifted. In her teens he sent her away
for long visits to friends in Scotland, which she enjoyed;
otherwise she grew up largely in London. Money was
always short in the family home.

When she was sixteen, Mary met Percy Bysshe Shelley. As a radical, a republican and an atheist, he was an enthusiastic admirer of her father, and he also revered the memory of her mother, approving her views on the status of women, marriage and divorce. For him, the discovery that these two great thinkers had produced a child as beautiful as she was intelligent was overwhelming. He was only twenty-two, with a wife, Harriet, and a small daughter; but within months, in the summer of 1814, Shelley and Mary eloped, leaving an outraged Godwin and a desperate Harriet, pregnant with her second child.

Mary's bliss lasted barely beyond the Channel crossing. Her first child, born prematurely, died. Shelley, although he had financial expectations as the son of a rich baronet, was tied in a tangle of debts and quarrels with his family, his wife's family and now Godwin also. Mary's stepsister, Claire Clairmont, had become part of their household, and Shelley's devotion to her, and her dependence on him, were a perpetual irritant. Claire involved herself briefly with Byron and became pregnant by him, but it was always Shelley who made himself responsible for her welfare, and many people believed that Mary and Claire shared his sexual attentions; and it was true that Shelley believed in sexual freedom, and at one point proposed to share Mary with his best friend from Oxford.

So far, their affairs were merely muddled, but in 1816, when Mary was writing *Frankenstein*, the horrors of life began to vie with those of her imagination. Her half-sister Fanny, depressed and neglected, committed suicide.

Almost immediately after this Shelley's wife Harriet drowned herself, leaving two small children whose custody her family was determined to retain. Shelley married Mary, albeit reluctantly, in the hope of winning custody of his children by Harriet, but failed to do so. He and Mary left for Italy in 1818 with their two children, accompanied by Claire and her daughter by Byron, Allegra. Four years of high poetic achievement and bitter sorrow followed; their children died, and Mary fell into deep depression, which was not dissipated by the birth of another child at the end of 1819. This was the broad background against which *Maurice*, written in the summer of 1820, had to be read.

III

Casa Cini, the home of the Dazzis, is in the centre of San Marcello, and well known to all the inhabitants, as we found when we set off to find it in the morning. It is a large, ancient family house, once famous for its hundred rooms, and still a maze of passages and winding stairs opening into surprising spaces, with paintings, sculptures and books everywhere. The family now occupy only a small part of the Casa, but they have preserved the family archives. It was among these archives that Cristina Dazzi came on Mary Shelley's story, while searching for something quite different at the request of the University of Pisa – papers connected with the poet Giacomo Leopardi, who became a friend of Lady Mountcashell and her daughters a few years after the Shelleys' stay in Pisa.

We were greeted by Andrea and Cristina Dazzi, and offered coffee. Then the manuscript of *Maurice* was brought out and laid in front of me on the table: an alarming moment, because coffee and manuscripts must not occupy the same space. Once we had separated them, I found *Maurice* exactly as Cristina Dazzi had described it.

The first thing to say about it is that it is an intrinsically attractive object, beautifully written and put together by someone who knew how to delight a child. From a more technical standpoint, the handwriting is easily legible and shows the characteristic letter formations of Mary Shelley. Catherine Payling compared it with other Mary Shelley manuscripts she had brought from the Keats–Shelley Museum, and we both felt there was no doubt of its being the same hand. Later Nora Crook was able to examine *Maurice* and do what I had not dared, given the fragility of the manuscript, which was to check the watermarks; after drawing on the researches of Dr Bruce Barker-Benfield of the Bodleian, she confirmed that the paper was of the same kind as that used by the Shelleys during their time in Pisa in 1820 and 1821.

The manuscript is divided into two booklets, the whole work only thirty-nine pages long. I read it through as fast as I could, taking a few notes, and copying out only a phrase here and there. Seeing a text for the first time, your brain races as you read. I was trying to relate it to Mary Shelley's other work. I was looking for her literary sources.

I was thinking about the circumstances of her life in 1820. I was trying to remember what I knew about Laurette and her family. At the same time, I wanted to read it purely as a piece of writing – to enjoy it as simply as Laurette must have enjoyed it.

Some of my first impressions follow. I noticed that the slim little story is divided into three parts, just like a three-volume adult novel of its time; and I guessed this was a playful touch, intended to please a bookish child. It mimics adult novels of the time in another way too, by giving the narrative to several different voices (like *Frankenstein*). First a countryman sets the scene; then the boy Maurice speaks; next, an unnamed 'Traveller' tells his story. The Traveller also repeats the long confessional story he has heard from a sailor's wife, which is a crucial element of the plot.

Maurice is the story of a boy who is stolen as a two-year-old from his wealthy parents by a woman who has no child of her own and longs for one – this is the poor sailor's wife. She brings him up lovingly, but he dimly remembers his other life; and when her husband ill treats him, he runs away with the idea of supporting himself by his own efforts. He gets work on a farm, only to find he is not strong enough to be a labourer; and is turned away and reduced to utter wretchedness. Then for a while he finds refuge with an old fisherman, Barnet. Barnet is grieving for the death of his wife, who, old and infirm as she was, had read her Bible to the village children and told them stories and ballads, *Goody Two-shoes* and 'Chevy Chase'. She was the

9

one person in this poor community who put them in touch with the world of the imagination, something outside their meagre lives: a reminder that Mary Shelley was the daughter of a woman who taught children and cared for the condition of the poor. But Maurice too reads the Bible and cries over the stories of Joseph and Absalom, which he can distantly relate to his own experience, and to brood on the histories of great men.

The modest idyll does not last. Barnet dies, and the cottage, which Maurice has come to love, is reclaimed. He is destitute again, and saved only when chance brings his true father, who has been searching for him for years, to discover him and restore him to an easier life.

Maurice is given a natural delicacy and goodness which is unaffected by the harsh conditions in which he is placed; he remains honest, well mannered and ready to trust people through all his ordeals. In *Frankenstein* Mary Shelley suggested that nurture, not nature, made the monster bad; it is an important point that impresses readers. Here she seems to be saying something different, by showing a child whose innate goodness survives ill-treatment. Maurice does not seek revenge; if anything he becomes gentler and more careful not to be led into cruelty of any kind himself. He has enough understanding even to forgive the woman who stole him from his sleeping nurse.

Although the story is called *Maurice*, this is not his real name. It is one he chooses for himself, to escape detection when he runs away from the sailor and his wife. His real name is Henry. As far as I know, Maurice is used nowhere else in Mary's work, but Henry was one of the most popular names of the period, and she had already given it to Victor Frankenstein's best friend, Henry Clerval. It was also used by her mother Mary Wollstonecraft for the hero of her first novel, and by Shelley in 1819 in his poem *Rosalind and Helen*.[2] This particular Henry, however, becomes attached to his name of Maurice. He makes a point of using it when he revisits his poor friends, as though to demonstrate that, even in his days of good fortune, he continues to value his other self and the memories of his other life of poverty. The fact that he is 'Maurice' in the title supports this loyalty to the poor and the past.

Some of Shelley's views surface in the narrative: a shopkeeper is a heartless and 'money loving man', reflecting his dislike of the mercantile classes. And Maurice, like Shelley, disapproves of people who shoot birds; this, and his decision not to catch fish because he wishes neither to destroy nor to give pain to living things, is a straight echo of Shelley's creed. On the other hand I was stopped short when I came to the passage in which Maurice is sent to Eton by his true father. What about Shelley's famously unhappy experience of being teased and bullied at his old school? True, he also had cheerful memories of summer picnics on the river at Eton, which he revived in 1821 in 'The Boat on the Serchio'. And Laurette's father was another Etonian; perhaps that was enough to make it the obvious school for Henry in Mary's mind.[3]

The setting of *Maurice*, mainly the south coast of Devon, appears nowhere else in Mary Shelley's writing. Torquay,

Sidmouth, Exeter and Plymouth are all mentioned; she must have been drawing on her memories of the visit she and Shelley made to south Devon in 1815. It was one of the few periods they ever spent on their own, and no doubt memorable for that reason.[4] Ilfracombe, on the north coast, also figures in the story (Mary first wrote 'Teignmouth' but substituted 'Ilfracombe'). Shelley was there in 1812 with Harriet, and Claire stayed close to it, alone, in 1815, but Mary never visited it, as far as we know; and we can read what we like into Mary making it the place from which Henry is stolen, as well as the native town of his cruel foster-father.

Maurice has a formally happy ending, but what struck me most at this first reading was its melancholy. It starts with a funeral and finishes with the crumbling away of the cottage that has sheltered Maurice. The theme is loss: parents lose their child and seek him year after year; another woman longs for a child so badly that she steals him; the child loses his identity when he changes his name, and is passed through the hands of three sets of parents, his natural ones, his foster-mother and old Barnet, who takes him in and then dies, leaving him alone and unprotected. Even writing for a child, Mary Shelley could not escape her melancholy.

There was no more time to read or reflect. The Dazzis offered to show us their library, and we followed them eagerly down to the great shuttered and chilly rooms on the *piano nobile*, lined with shelves crammed to the high ceilings with books of four centuries. First editions of *Adonais* and *Epipsychidion* were placed on a table. The packing case in which Mary Shelley's story had lain for so long stood behind a door.

Before leaving, I was taken to meet Signora Dazzi senior. Her English is perfect, and her memories go back to the early years of this century. She told me that she remembered the husband of Laurette very well, and that his white beard had frightened her as a small child. Could she really mean Laurette's husband, I asked myself? She did. Placido Tardy was Laurette's second husband, a Sicilian who became a professor of mathematics in Genoa; when I returned to San Marcello I found many photographs of him in family albums, confirming that he had lived to be ninety-eight, dying in 1914, thirty-four years after his wife.

This first visit to San Marcello was as intense as it was brief. I had to read and respond to *Maurice* fast. At the same time I was made aware that the family's links with what I thought of as the distant past were much closer than I had imagined. Signora Dazzi senior is the great-granddaughter of Laurette's sister Nerina Tighe and her Italian husband, Bartolomeo Cini; we were in the house to which Nerina came as a bride in 1834, and where her friend Claire Clairmont was also made welcome. Here Nerina's son, Gianni Cini, born in 1840, lived until 1930. Outside the windows of Casa Cini a romantic garden partly planned by Nerina still covers the hillside above the house, with grottoes and fountains rising high in the air, a vast stone-built summer house like a small palace, an ice house and a now decaying rose arbour; the yew trees were planted in honour of Nerina's Irish parentage. A later generation put in a sunken tennis court that was flooded in winter for skating, and used the descending water courses to power an early electricity supply. Thoughts of Henry James, Edward Silsbee and *The Aspern Papers* came into my head; and indeed, American collectors had been here in the 1960s and carried off some of the Cini archive. We were the second wave of barbarians, but now the family had no wish to sell anything; rather, a strong desire to retain their precious inheritance and make it accessible to all visiting scholars.

IV

Maurice was produced at the high tide of Romanticism. Mary had already published *Frankenstein*. She had also written a startling novel of father–daughter incest, *Matilda*, a few months before *Maurice*; her father, not surprisingly, advised her against publishing *Matilda*.[5] Shelley was in the full flight of his inspiration, dividing his energies between political and lyrical writing. Byron, also in Italy, had published the first two cantos of *Don Juan* and was working on the next. Keats's odes appeared in print that summer of 1820, and Shelley wrote to him in London, inviting him to join them in Italy; and Keats, knowing himself to be dying of tuberculosis, began to plan a journey to Rome.

From Mary Shelley's account of 1820 we know that she and Shelley also read and admired Wordsworth of the older generation of Romantic poets. 'No man ever admired Wordsworth's poetry more – he read it perpetually, and taught others to appreciate its beauties,' she says; and Wordsworth does seem to preside over *Maurice*, with its clear, straightforward language and its setting among simple people and poor labourers, and against elemental backgrounds of rocks and trees, cliffs and seashore.[6] Like Wordsworth, Mary delights in describing the moss and lichens ('yellow, green, white & blue') growing on an old thatched roof, and the wallflowers and honeysuckle round a cottage; and she puts in finely observed detail, such as the way the sea becomes invisible to watchers on the beach when the sky turns dark. Her story is entirely unlike the moral and educational tales popular with publishers and parents of that date (and the staple of her father's publishing firm), directing young readers to the social virtues and away from the vices of vanity, lying and cruelty. *Maurice* has no designs on the reader; it simply tells a human tale, and arouses human sympathy.

It is a small work, but touched with the same spirit as the greater ones it stands among. It takes the experience of a child who loses his identity and finds himself isolated in a hostile world. For him, the fisherman's cottage of the title becomes a symbol of security and love; and on the last pages, although he is restored to his true place and name, he sees the cottage destroyed by the natural forces of wind, weather and time. The themes of the story are romantic: the vulnerability of childhood, and of parent-hood; displacement, loss, pain, death and rehabilitation; delight in the natural world; and the power of time both to heal and to destroy.

By a stroke of fate, the history of the manuscript of *Maurice* also embodies some of these same romantic themes. The fragile object, lost for many decades, was found again quite unexpectedly, still within the same family to which it was presented. It came to light in a great and ancient house in the Apennines, itself also threatened by time and change, although preserving in its core a unique collection of family papers, books, documents, letters and poems. Through this archive, and through the story, the life of the early nine-teenth century has been kept alive; past and present co-exist.

V

To begin with, there is the matter of lost children. You have only to look at the two households involved in Mary Shelley's gift of *Maurice* to Laurette – the Irish household of the Tighes and the English household of the Shelleys – and make the tally of children lost to each of them, to see how Mary's imagination came to settle on such a theme.

The Shelley household in 1820 consisted of three adults, the poet Percy Bysshe, his wife Mary and his stepsister Claire Clairmont, all in their twenties; with the addition of the Shelleys' infant son Percy Florence. The Tighe household consisted of two adults in their mid-forties, George Tighe and his consort, known either as Lady Mountcashell (her real name) or Mrs Mason (her assumed name), and their two young daughters, ten-year-old Laurette, or Laura, and four-year-old Nerina. On the surface, two complete and happy families; but nothing was as it appeared. Margaret Mountcashell had seven older children who were lost to her. On separating from her husband she had been forced to give them up; the law gave her no right to them at all. Her family with George Tighe was a second start, begun in her mid-thirties; and Laurette and Nerina were brought up to understand that they 'could never expect to be acknowledged by any of their mother's relations'.[7]

The Shelleys were haunted in the same way. Ianthe and Charles, Shelley's children by Harriet, were being brought up by guardians appointed by the Court of Chancery; they were five and three years old when he left England. The three children born to him and Mary in 1815, 1816 and 1817 had died one after another, the first within a few weeks of her birth, Clara aged one in Venice and William aged three in Rome. The next child missing from the household was Claire's three-year-old daughter Allegra, and it is Allegra's fate that was most agonizing during 1820. Claire had given Allegra up to Byron, her father, believing this to be in the best interest of her child, with a promise that she should be allowed to visit her. Now he was denying Claire visits and failing to keep her informed of Allegra's whereabouts or health; for six months in 1819 no word of any kind came from him or his servants.

There is still one more child to be noticed. Elena Adelaide Shelley was registered by Shelley in Naples early in 1819 as his own and Mary's newborn daughter, and – almost unbelievably – left in Naples when they set off for Rome, to be collected later. She was not Mary's child, and she was never collected, because in the spring of 1820 she fell ill, and in June she died. She is the seventh lost child of the Shelley household.[8]

When you consider that each family counted seven lost children, Mary's use of a child stolen from its parents as the central figure in her story begins to look like an allusion, conscious or not, to the grief, fear, remorse and mourning of both families. Another likely element was her own history as a child who had lost her mother at birth, and acquired a disliked stepmother. Claire too had never known her father, or even his identity. Shelley was estranged from his family; Margaret Mountcashell from hers. To the righteous in England, the Tighes and the Shelleys appeared as the morally dispossessed, taking refuge together in Italy; to themselves, as parents and as children, they must have felt a peculiarly vulnerable group.

VI

After I read *Maurice* I determined to find out everything I could about Laurette, her parents and her history. To begin with, how did an Irish family come to be settled in

Italy in 1820? Their story takes us back into the eighteenth century, and there is comedy as well as tragedy in this piece of domestic history. Laurette's mother began life as the Honourable Margaret King, daughter of a viscount, later an earl. In 1786, when she was fourteen, she had a governess who impressed her deeply: Mary Wollstonecraft, whose 'mind appeared more noble & her understanding more cultivated than any others I had known', and who went on to write her great statement of women's rights and to be known as a supporter of radical social reform.[9] So the families were already linked a generation earlier. Margaret King approved and followed many of her governess's views, even after she became a countess through her marriage to the young Earl of Mountcashell.

She thought she could rule her husband, and found she could not. Their politics were opposed, he a Tory, she a republican and democrat, like her governess. She was a supporter – necessarily discreet – of the rising of the United Irishmen in 1798 and was grieved by its failure. When this was followed by the English government's imposition of the Act of Union, dooming Ireland to impotence and aggravating its poverty, she despaired for her country.

She was also dissatisfied with her personal situation. She wanted to do more than give birth to a child every eighteen months and preside over her husband's great house on St Stephen's Green in Dublin or his country mansion in County Cork. She was interested in writing – had written a couple of political pamphlets – and in the study of medicine, although it was closed to women.

In 1801 she persuaded her husband to take a continental tour. The ending of the war between England and France made travel easier than it had been for a decade, and, although she and the Earl agreed on few points, he had no objection to spending his rents on a fashionable Grand Tour. They set off in the style required of their rank and fortune, with a couple of coaches, a woman friend to keep the Countess company, four servants and five children, tutor and governess. First they went to London, where they stayed for two months in the autumn of 1801. Margaret could not visit her former governess, since she had died in childbirth in 1797, but she could and did call on her widower, William Godwin; they had previously met in Dublin in 1800, and exchanged letters.

Godwin and Margaret Mountcashell shared an interest in child-rearing and education, and she knew he was struggling to care for Mary Wollstonecraft's two daughters, four-year-old Mary and seven-year-old Fanny. 'It would give me great pleasure to see your two little girls,' she wrote in advance of her visit; and it seems likely that the first meeting between Margaret Mountcashell and Mary Godwin (later Shelley) took place at this time.[10] Godwin described his aristocratic friend as handsome but also brawny, with 'gigantic arms, which she commonly folds, naked and exposed almost up to the shoulders'.[11] She did not care about fashion; but she was clever and well read, with the self-confidence bordering on imperiousness of an aristocrat, in spite of her democratic opinions. And she was very tall, with brilliant blue eyes; altogether a striking creature.

At the end of November the Mountcashells proceeded to Paris, where they visited the sights and were received by the Bonapartes. They gave receptions for all their new acquaintances, from Talleyrand, Lafayette and the painter David to Charles James Fox, Tom Paine, John Kemble, Amelia Opie, Thomas Holcroft and Helen Maria Williams, many of whom had been friends of Mary Wollstonecraft.[12]

During this long stay in Paris, Margaret gave birth to another son, Richard. In September 1802 they travelled on to Italy, where, after months in Naples, Rome and Florence, Margaret fell ill. By the time she was better, war had broken out again between England and France, blocking their homeward journey. They returned to Rome; she was pregnant again. This would be her eighth child, one having died in infancy; but now in Rome her life changed course. A sheaf of poems in her hand, some inscribed 'Rome 1804 M. M.', show her overwhelmed by a new experience. She fell in love. She writes of a 'bright dream', of 'romantic visions', of a man who has 'taught my heart unknown delights', and 'made me prove each fine degree/From joyful love to maddening jealousy'. 'Would thou couldst feel a passion strong as mine,' she urges him. 'Beloved beyond existence, health or fame.'[13]

The man she addressed was George Tighe. He was at first a friend of her husband. They had the common background of the Anglo-Irish Ascendancy, and Tighe was an Etonian; but he was not rich, had no title or great position in society, and had inherited as many debts as

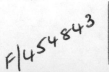

acres of Irish land. He was, however, a poet and a classical scholar. He had served as an officer in the mid-1790s, when so many young men took commissions in the militia raised to defend Britain from the French threat; then, finding himself heir to his father's estates, and at something of a loose end, he decided to see Italy. In Rome he joined a literary society, the Arcadi Pastori, of which Goethe was a member, and dreamed of the simple life.

Some of his poems have survived too, in which he addresses Margaret by the Petrarchan name of Laura. His Laura was a formidable mistress, four years older than him and a countess, rich and highly placed in society, as well as pregnant by her husband. Their mutual absorption was noticed by the Anglo-Irish community in Rome, and Lord Mountcashell's jealousy was aroused. At this stage Margaret did not intend to put her marriage at risk. After the birth of her third daughter, Elizabeth, in August 1804, she set off with her husband and family for the long return journey to Ireland.

France being enemy territory, their path lay through Germany; and in Germany she had second thoughts about continuing homewards. The Earl went ahead with the older boys, and she remained with her three daughters and Richard. By her own account, she had decided to go south again for her health before eventually returning to Ireland. She said nothing about Tighe, but it is clear from Tighe's papers and her own later statement that he joined her in Germany. They wandered from one place to another; there is mention of Dresden, Munich, Ratisbon, Carslbad, Eger

and Jena. The fact that Napoleon's armies were fighting all over the territory must have made things difficult and sometimes dangerous, even for a countess. In October 1805 the French defeated the Austrians at Ulm; it was the same month in which Nelson defeated the French navy at Trafalgar. In December Napoleon crushed the Austrians and the Russians at Austerlitz, and in October 1806 he did the same to the Prussian army at Jena.

Throughout this period Margaret and George Tighe were in Germany. She sent her two elder daughters and Richard back to England from Dresden in the summer of 1806, keeping baby Eliza with her. At this point Lord Mountcashell became angry and wrote 'ordering me to return to England immediately to sign articles of separation & to give up my youngest child to him, threatening in case of non-compliance to stop my remittances & to find means of taking the child by force'.[14]

His threats prompted her to write to her lawyer in Ireland, asking 'whether Lord M can take her [baby] from me by force (that is whether the law would authorize such a step) at her age, and whether I have only dreamt that a mother can keep her child with her in spite of the father till seven years old?'[15] She was prepared to fight for her youngest child, and said her heart ached when she thought of the others; and that she had no wish for a separation, 'as I should endure much for the sake of our children and indeed have done so for some years'. She was also careful to tell the lawyer, 'I hope soon to be in French territories (either Italy or France I am not sure which) and suppose it will not be in the power of anyone to molest me there – In perfect solitude and tranquillity I hope to recover my health – I shall seek no society.'[16]

Lord Mountcashell must have reasoned that she was effectively separating herself from him, and probably with her lover; and since he had control of the money he could dictate terms. For the moment, she and Tighe remained in Germany, living on credit. She later told her daughters that she followed medical lectures at Jena, disguising herself in men's clothes to gain admittance. Jena was renowned for its democratic student body, its openness to new ideas, a teaching faculty that included Hegel and Schiller, and an enlightened ruler who was Goethe's patron. A poem by Tighe describing the battle of Jena suggests he was there to witness the event.

Yet Tighe was in two minds about their future. One of her poems, written in Dresden in 1806, ends,

Why thought I madly of an equal flame,
When dying embers only seem to glow;
Where the exhausted spirit knows the name
Of Love; but passion's force forgets to know?
Vesuvius' self no longer is the same,
And soon the liquid fire must cease to flow.[17]

If Tighe was no longer a Vesuvius, two poems of his, written in Jena in September of the same year – just before the battle – give some account of his private conflict. The first appears to be ending his relationship with his Laura:

Yes, Laura, our summer is o'er
And chill blows the heart-piercing blast;
Alas must we also deplore
That the Summer of Love it is past?

. . . Thy fancys, caprices, & fears
No emotions but anger impart;
And the storms of reproaches & tears
Have wither'd this desolate heart.

But the second, 'Palinode' (which means recantation), is
intended to reassure:

Yes Laura our summer is o'er
But let us not mourn for the past;
If the blossoms of Love are no more
Let Friendship's fair ever-green last.

. . . No more shall thy fancys & fears
Emotions of anger impart:
Oh come let me wipe off those tears,
And press thee once more to my Heart.[18]

Reassured by Tighe, Margaret still had to face the battle
for custody of her children; and, having no legal rights,
she soon lost the youngest along with the others. As a
married woman she possessed nothing, and her brothers
did not offer to assist her, so that the Earl was able to force
her to comply by putting on financial pressure. In 1807

she was in London and then Dublin, which is probably where she handed over three-year-old Eliza; she never saw her again.

Her friend Lady Moira said she thought the Earl intended a divorce; and went on, 'I am convinced of her [Margaret Mountcashell's] uprightness and real purity of mind – but her minor errors as to judgement I cannot close my eyes upon.' Her 'frank & generous disposition' sometimes misled her, and although Lady Moira would not join with her 'enemies' and 'maligners', she had harsh things to say about Tighe. 'I am grieved to learn . . . that Mr Tighe, once Ld M C 's friend & favorite till he assumed & professed a jealousy of him, is a man of insignificance in every mental quality, & of a vanity to make a parade of being the cause of such a disagreement.'[19] There was no divorce, but the lovers were ostracized by Dublin and London society alike.

Margaret did, however, renew her friendship with William Godwin, now married to a Mrs Clairmont, and running their Juvenile Library in Holborn. At the end of the year they published Lady Mountcashell's *Stories of Old Daniel*: the book became one of the Juvenile Library's biggest successes, went into many editions and was followed by *Continuation of the Stories of Old Daniel*. It was not, of course, put out under Lady Mountcashell's name. She had in any case stopped using it. According to what she later told Claire Clairmont, this was at the insistence of Tighe; and, since he did not want her to take his name either, she chose to be called 'Mrs Mason', the name of the good governess in the children's stories by her own well-remembered governess, Mary Wollstonecraft.

Five years after the birth of Eliza Mountcashell, Mrs Mason bore a daughter to George Tighe, on 19 July 1809. The long gap may be a tribute to her medical knowledge; it certainly suggests they deliberated before allowing themselves a child to replace those lost to her. Anna Laura Georgina was always known as Laurette or Laura, her name surely an allusion to the Petrarchan poems her father wrote for her mother. Without a divorce, they could not marry; and it appears that Mrs Mason and Tighe were in Vienna for the birth, since Tighe had money sent to him there in 1810, and Laurette's obituary states that was where she was born. They were back in England by 1812; but when the Earl agreed to allow her £800 a year, and to settle the debts she had run up abroad, they decided to start another life in Italy.

In 1814 Europe was at peace again after the defeat of Napoleon. In March the Allies entered Paris, in May Louis XVIII followed, and in August Tighe, Mrs Mason and Laurette left England and travelled to Italy through France. Pisa was chosen as a quiet town with a university and a good medical school, sea and the mountains at hand, and not so far south as to be unbearably hot in summer. It is also close to Florence; but Florence would always be avoided by Mrs Mason, for fear of encountering English visitors. The Tighes took a house south of the River Arno, Casa Silva, and there in Pisa their second daughter was born on 20 June 1815. She was always known as Nerina, although her formal names were Catherine Elizabeth Raniera. Margaret watched over the second family with the most anxious attention; Laurette slept either in her room or next door to it, and she was unwilling to be separated from her.

Tighe remained a reader and occasional writer, and between them they collected an impressive library. He also took up agricultural studies, with a particular interest in cultivating potatoes, not at that time much appreciated in Tuscany; in the family he was known as 'Tatty'. Friends at home got him a Civil List pension of £400 a year, and he had another £200 from his Irish rents, so that by local standards Mr Tighe and Mrs Mason were rich. She continued to be interested in medicine, and did good work among the poor of Pisa, dispensing medicines and good advice.

He was a loving father, but both he and Mrs Mason were ambivalent about what they had done, as his account makes clear: 'after many storms we now enjoy as much happiness as falls to the lot of most people. But let it be remembered that this has been gained after many years of doubt and anxiety & that generally speaking an illegitimate connection is as miserable as it is criminal.'[20] She ended a note written for her daughters in 1818 with the warning words quoted earlier, insisting that they could never expect to be acknowledged by any of her relations. Her statement shows how absolute was the social rejection brought by her adultery, and how entirely she accepted it; in the same note she wrote, 'Misfortune must ever be the lot of those who transgress the laws of social life.'[21] More cheerfully, she welcomed her escape from the aristocracy and her new position 'in that middle rank of life for which I always sighed'.[22]

Neither she nor Tighe returned to England, and at what point Laurette and Nerina became aware of the existence of their seven half-brothers and sisters is not clear. They grew up speaking and writing English and Italian with equal fluency, but never visited England or Ireland; and when Laurette decided to become a novelist and essayist she chose to write in Italian.

VII

The year in which George Tighe and Margaret Mountcashell left England for Italy, 1814, was also the year in which Mary Godwin ran away from their parents' house in Holborn and crossed the Channel with the poet Shelley and her stepsister Claire. The three of them – the girls hardly more than children – had worked themselves into a state in which they were oblivious of everything but their mutual intoxication. They made their first trip together across France, through Switzerland and back down the Rhine. They returned to England to face severe difficulties. Both Shelley's wife Harriet and Mary were now pregnant, and he was pursued by creditors. Harriet bore a son, Charles, who lived. Mary's child, a premature daughter, died at a few weeks. A summary must do for the well-known facts that follow. In 1816 Mary had a son, William; very soon after this Claire entangled herself with Byron. If she was silly, he was careless; she pursued him and was soon pregnant. She remained, however, a part of the Shelley household. In 1816 they summered with Byron on the shores of Lac Léman, where the idea of *Frankenstein* came to Mary. That autumn saw the suicides of Fanny and Harriet.

Claire's daughter Allegra was loved by Shelley as much as his own children, and William and Allegra were play-mates in their shared household; indeed, despite Mary's resentment at Claire's presence, the children of the double family were equally loved by them all. Mary's daughter Clara was born in September 1817, and early in 1818 they all set off for Italy together. Shelley hoped his health would improve in a southern climate, and the plan was that the Shelleys' Swiss maid Elise should take Allegra to Byron in Venice. He had agreed to be responsible for her upbring-ing, and, painful as this was to Claire, she believed it would give her child the best chance in life, as the acknowledged daughter of a peer. 'I have sent you my child because I love her too well to keep her,' she wrote to him.[23] Heartbreaking words.

Allegra, fifteen months old and never before parted from her mother, was sent to Byron in Venice in April 1818. As the summer went by, Claire became worried about her, getting scant news from Elise, but learning that she had been put into the care of the British Consul, Richard Hoppner and his Swiss wife. Mrs Hoppner wrote coolly to Mary Shelley about Allegra wetting her bed and losing her gaiety of spirit.[24] As the acknowledged daughter of a peer she was important; her unhappiness as a child was not. In August Claire asked Shelley to take her to Venice to see Allegra. Mary stayed behind at Bagni di Lucca, but when Shelley met Byron he told him the whole family party was with him. Byron allowed Allegra to go to her mother, and lent them his villa at Este; and Shelley had to send for Mary to come at all speed to make his story stand up. Mary set off; baby Clara was not well, and the journey did not improve her condition. After two weeks at Este, they decided to take her to a doctor in Venice; by the time they reached Venice, Clara was dying.

Clara was buried, Claire looking after Allegra and William. She was allowed to keep Allegra with her until the end of October, when Byron insisted on having her back. The Shelleys then travelled south with Claire. Mary was sunk in depression; perhaps she held Shelley and Claire partly responsible for the death of Clara. Shelley was also depressed.

As we have seen, Shelley registered the birth of another daughter to himself and Mary that winter in Naples, Elena Adelaide, giving her birth date as 27 December 1818. Mary appears to have known nothing about her at this stage, and no one has yet given a satisfactory explanation of her parentage.[25] The Shelleys moved to Rome, leaving Elena in the care of a humble family, and intending to return. In Rome they suffered their most devastating blow yet when three-year-old William died after a few days' illness. Mary had now lost all three of her children. As she wrote at the beginning of her new journal in August 1819, 'to have won & then cruelly have lost the associations of four years is not an accident to which the human mind can bend without much suffering'.[26] Her depression darkened, and never entirely lifted again; Shelley spoke of it as a form of torture which she inflicted on him as well as on herself.

Claire grieved with Mary and Shelley; and she had a further cause for misery in Byron's refusal to allow visits or to keep her informed about Allegra's whereabouts or health. She grew frightened for her daughter.

The only gleam of hope among them was that Mary was pregnant again. Her child was due in November, and they agreed that Florence would be a good place for the birth. On their way to Florence they stopped in Pisa and took a letter of introduction from Godwin to Lady Mountcashell – or rather, Mrs Mason; and in this way Mary Wollstonecraft's pupil became the friend of the daughter Mary Wollstonecraft never knew.

With such links the two families were well disposed towards one another. Friendship sprang up at once. The Tighes had their library to share with the Shelleys; like them, they devoted much of their time to reading classical and modern literature. Tighe and Margaret were poets and writers, as the Shelleys were. Both groups considered themselves democrats, republicans and free-thinkers; the Tighes had a supply of subversive political pamphlets from England, and there were borrowings and lendings on both sides. Finally, both families were refugees from the intense disapproval of their compatriots.

Four remarkable women are linked in the creation of *Maurice* by Mary Shelley (*lower left*). Her mother, Mary Wollstonecraft (*top left*), the radical writer, had been governess to the aristocratic Margaret King, later Countess Mountcashell (*top right*). She too became a writer, and befriended her governess's daughter in Italy, where *Maurice* was written for Lady Mountcashell's daughter Laurette (*lower right*). Laurette in her turn also became a writer.

Mary Shelley had small support from her father, William Godwin (*top left*), who chided her for grieving for her dead children and rejected *Maurice* for publication; or from her husband, Shelley (*top right*), who turned to other women, often preferring the company of her step-sister Claire Clairmont (*lower left*), mother of Allegra by Byron (*lower right*).

Two of the lost children who lie behind *Maurice*. William (*above*), cherished son of Mary and Shelley, died of a fever in Rome in 1819. His equally beloved playmate, Allegra (*below*), was entrusted to Byron by Claire in the belief that it would be for the child's ultimate good. Byron then refused to allow Claire visits and neglected even to keep her informed about Allegra's health and whereabouts. Mary Shelley described his behaviour as remorseless and cruel, with good reason, since Allegra died at the age of five in the convent to which Byron had sent her, unvisited by him and wilfully denied her mother's loving presence.

dess: aussi grandeur et gravé par Quenedey rue neuve des petits champs n.º 1284 à Paris

Lady Mountcashell in Paris in 1802, embarked on a Grand Tour with her husband the Earl and their children. During the course of the tour she bore him two more children, but in Rome she fell in love with another Irish gentleman, William Tighe, and separated from the Earl. Although she battled to keep her younger children at least with her, the Earl gained custody and she was permanently separated from them. Her two illegitimate daughters by Tighe, Laurette and Nerina, were anxiously and devotedly watched over, and grew up adoring their mother.

Ostracized by English and Irish society, Tighe and Lady Mountcashell –
now calling herself 'Mrs Mason' – settled in Pisa, where the university
provided a congenial intellectual environment.

Their younger daughter,
Nerina, married a Tuscan
landowner, Bartolomeo Cini,
whose large house in the
Apennines became a centre
for the extended family and
friends.

A photograph of Laurette in the late 1840s (*above*). Her first marriage to a scoundrelly Corsican diplomat, Adolphe Galloni, was a disaster, and at about this time she separated from him and started writing novels, encouraged by a sympathetic Mary Shelley. But Laurette seems not to have introduced Mary to her Sicilian lover, Placido Tardy (*below*), whom she was able to marry only after Galloni's death in 1853. Tardy was a distinguished mathematician and supporter of Cavour in the struggle for Italian unification, and he became Rector of the University of Genoa in 1865.

Laurette in later life, established as a journalist and novelist under the name 'Sara' (*above*). She remained childless, but she and Professor Tardy (*below*) were close to Nerina and Bartolomeo Cini and their children. After Laurette's death in 1880, Tardy made his home with the Cinis. This is how Laurette's papers – including the manuscript of *Maurice* – came to the Cini house. The Professor lived to the age of ninety-eight, dying in 1914, and is still vividly remembered in the family.

Lady Mountcashell in 1835, shortly before her death, painted by her sister
Diana. On the back are the pencilled words 'Diana King fecit 1835'
followed by 'Elle ne vit plus que dans nos coeurs'. Below this is her name
'Margaret Jane Countess Dow/r of Mount Cashel'.

Claire later described Mrs Mason as possessed of a 'lofty and calm presence', and always cheerful – unlike both Byron and Shelley, she added; and Laurette and Nerina were delighted to have new friends in Mary, Claire and Shelley, who responded warmly to the children.[27] The Shelleys went on to Florence, from which Mary wrote to Mrs Mason praising Laurette's 'simplicity and frankness', and Mrs Mason wrote back that Laurette wanted to know whether 'that lady had yet *made her child*'.[28] After the birth on 11 November, Mrs Mason wrote congratulating them, with messages from her daughters: 'Your kind remembrance of Laurette flatters her parents extremely – she is rejoiced to hear of the birth of the little child, which she longs to see, and desires me to tell you to come here soon.' Laurette also was practising the pianoforte with more than usual attention in hopes of 'amazing' the musical Claire, and 'my little Nerina often asks "*Dove son quegli Signori Inglesi?*"'[29]

Mary and Shelley's child, Percy Florence, was born without trouble. He was small but vigorous, and Mary fed him herself. It was Shelley who grumbled about his own health, with a pain in his side – that standard nineteenth-century complaint – and occasional fevers. They did not stop him writing: the 'Ode to the West Wind' was composed in Florence that autumn. Then the weather turned bitter – *scellerato* and *stravagantissimo* weather, Mrs Mason called it – and the winter of 1819/20 became the coldest Tuscany had experienced for seventy years. Tighe was also afflicted with rheumatism, and kept to his bed in

Pisa. In spite of the weather, and difficulties with servants, when Mary's baby was two months old she invited Laurette to come and stay in Florence. Mrs Mason's reply, dated 14 January, was an apologetic refusal: 'You will perhaps think me very weak when I confess to you that, accustomed as I am to have her always sleeping in my room or the next to it, I fear when on wakening in the night should recollect that she was far from me, it would at this moment have too strong an effect on my shattered nerves.'[30] When Laurette was older she might stay with them, but for the moment she could not be parted from her. The serenity and good spirits noted by Claire were evidently not the whole picture.

On 26 January 1820, after what Claire described mysteriously as a 'half baptism' for Percy Florence, the Shelleys moved by boat and carriage to Pisa, where they took a house. 'Walk with – S – about the town seeking Lodgings. Call on Mrs Mason and the pretty Laurette – The Weather most exquisitely warm & sunny – Read an Irish pamphlet,' wrote Claire in her diary the next day.[31] After this she was in and out of Casa Silva, becoming more intimate with the family than Mary and acting like an elder sister to Laurette. She walked and rode with her on the banks of the Arno, took her to enjoy the Carnival festivities and went with her to the opera several times, to hear Rossini's *Cenerentola* on one occasion and the renowned soprano Angelica Catalani on another. Mr Tighe was less in evidence; Claire did not meet him until the end of April. Meanwhile baby Percy caught a light case of measles from

four-year-old Nerina, and both quickly recovered. Mrs
Mason advised Mary about the hiring of servants and the
importance of keeping calm while nursing a baby; she also
expressed her admiration of *Frankenstein*. She told Claire
stories of her past, and discussed politics with Shelley. She
even wrote an admiring humorous poem about him,
'Twelve Cogent Reasons for Supposing P. B. Sh–ll–y to be
the D–v–l Inc–rn–t–', listing his devilish qualities – sensi-
tivity, tolerance, linguistic ability, charity to the poor, a
preference for justice rather than wealth (the text appears as
the Appendix, pp. 137–41). He in turn wrote 'The Sensitive
Plant', which some think alluded to Mrs Mason's garden.

That summer of 1820 the Shelleys were moving between
Pisa, the nearby spa of San Giuliano, and Livorno, where
they were lent a house by English friends, the Gisbornes.
They enjoyed the sea coast, with its dramatically changing
skies and myrtle hedges full of fireflies. Shelley wrote his
'To a Skylark' at Livorno. He turned to satire, with an eye
on English politics and George IV's undignified struggle
to rid himself of Queen Caroline: the verse drama *Swellfoot
the Tyrant*, with its chorus of pigs, was the result. He began
a prose *Philosophical View of Reform*, in which he attacked
the merchant aristocracy of England and urged the poor
to protest. Mary got on with research into the history of
a prince of the neighbouring town of Lucca for a historical
novel, *Valperga*.

At the end of April Claire wrote to Byron in Ravenna,
asking to have Allegra for the summer – she had not seen
her for eighteen months – and pointing out that the child's

health had already suffered from the climate and conditions of eastern Italy. 'Though I can scarcely believe it possible you will refuse my just requests yet I beg you to remember that I did not part with her at Milan until I had received your formal & explicit declaration that I should see my child at proper intervals.' The postscript reads, 'Pray kiss my dear child many times for me.'[32] Byron sent a roughly worded message that he would not let Allegra go to the Shelley household, citing its bad record for child mortality (nor, he added, did he wish her to 'be taught to believe that there is no Deity'). Claire wrote again, offering to take Allegra on her own: 'This letter is an appeal to your Justice . . . I have exerted myself to remove your objections & my claim is bare & obvious . . . I can find no words to express my gratitude to all those who have been kind to my Allegra.'[33]

On 4 May she drafted another letter, urging him not to put Allegra into a convent, as he now threatened. So the months went by, Claire pleading, Byron ignoring her pleas. He could not stomach her having any claim on his attention or their child; besides this, he was absorbed in his love affair with Countess Teresa Guiccioli. Mary was impatient with Claire, and still jealous of her share of Shelley's love, so that they quarrelled regularly; but she could not be unaware of her suffering. And for all Mary's ambivalence about Claire, the shadow of Allegra falls as closely on her story of a child ill-used, and longed for by a loving parent, as the memory of her own lost William.

The tangle of tragedies knots tighter. Shelley heard that

Elena was ill in Naples, and wrote to their friends the Gisbornes saying he expected her to die; her memory would torture him, he said. The Shelleys' former maid Elise and her Italian husband began a blackmail attempt, alleging that Elena was Claire's child by Shelley. With the help of a lawyer, he put off the blackmail attempt. Then came news of Elena's death.

None of the Shelley household could be content, but Claire at least had her consoling friendship with Mrs Mason and her family. In July she was reading Mrs Mason's *Continuation of the Stories of Old Daniel*.[34] She spent Laurette's eleventh birthday with her in Pisa. The next day they rode to Livorno to spend the day with Mary, setting off at five in the morning, and making an expedition along the coast. This is the likely spark for Mary's story for Laurette, set on a different sea coast. Three weeks later Laurette was presented with *Maurice*, perhaps as a late birthday present.[35]

The manuscript is clearly a fair copy, with very few second thoughts. At some point Mary made another copy, which she submitted to her father; his rejection was the last of it as far as she was concerned. Nor is there any mention of it in any papers of Laurette's that I have seen; but there can be no doubt that she prized it and kept it among her treasures. As she grew up, she began to write herself; later she asked advice and help of Mary Shelley, whose example and success as a writer, alongside that of her mother, encouraged her to follow the same path.

VIII

The two families maintained their friendship over the next two years. Mary's letters remain cheerless. It could hardly have been otherwise. She was arranging a gravestone for William in Rome, tending her remaining son, and working at her novel. In her spare time she took Greek lessons. Claire, advised by Mrs Mason, went to Florence, lodging with the family of Dr Antonio Bojti, physician and friend to the Grand Duke Ferdinand; his German mother-in-law gave Claire German lessons, while she taught the Bojti children English. She was industrious but could not be happy, and her diary records her hopes and dreams of being allowed to see her child again, and her perpetual disappointment.

News of the death of Keats in Rome brought sorrow to them all. Shelley wrote his lament *Adonais*, in which he seems to be mourning his own fate as much as that of Keats. Missing Claire, he interested himself in other women, first Emilia Viviani, kept in a convent by her parents, then Jane Williams, who arrived with her lover in Pisa in 1821.

In March 1821 Claire learnt that Byron, breaking another promise, had placed Allegra in a convent. She was the youngest child to be admitted. When Shelley visited the convent without telling Claire, he was worried enough by what he saw to ask Mary, 'Do you think Mrs Mason could be prevailed upon to *propose* to take charge of her?' He added, 'I fear not,' and no more was heard of the idea.[36] And although he called Mr Tighe 'seriously my friend', Shelley was now in two minds about Mrs Mason, whom he described as annoyingly perverse, perhaps because she had too much influence over Claire and encouraged her to seek an independent life.

When Byron came to Pisa in November 1821, he and Shelley drew close again. Shelley found his charm irresistible, but he did not introduce him to the Tighes, and Tighe is said to have referred to Byron as Bluebeard, or Henry VIII. Claire, in Florence, became desperate about Allegra's isolation from both her parents. She thought of kidnapping her, and later said Lady Mountcashell had offered to give her the means to emigrate to Australia with her child. The Shelleys urged her to continue to accept the convent placing in the hope that Byron would presently lose interest in his daughter. 'Nothing remains constant, something may happen – things cannot be worse,' wrote Mary to Claire.[37] If she meant to be kind in advising Claire, assuring her that the convent was healthy, she also conceded that Byron's 'hypocrisy & cruelty rouse one's soul from its depths' and that 'as soon as possible A. ought to be taken out of the hands of one as remorseless as he is unprincipled'.[38] Yet the Shelleys did nothing.

Claire's last plea to Byron was made in February 1822. 'My dear Friend, I conjure you do not make the world dark to me, as if my Allegra were dead. In the happiness her sight will cause me I shall gain restoration and strength to enable me to bear the mortifications and displeasures to which a poor and unhappy person is exposed in the world. I wish you every happiness.'[39] She got no answer, and in April she expressed her disquiet about Allegra's health to Mary: 'I fear she is sick.'[40] Within two weeks, her child was dead.[41]

Claire responded to the news with the dignity of someone who has nothing more to fear. A few weeks later Shelley was dead too, drowned while sailing off the coast. Mary and Claire were both now without protection or money, since Shelley's allowance stopped, there was doubt about the legality of his will, and without a will his son Charles was his heir. Claire set off almost at once for Vienna, where her brother was, to seek work, only to find that her connection with Shelley and Byron made her suspect to Metternich's police; no one would employ her, and she fell seriously ill. Hearing of this, Mrs Mason wrote to Byron to suggest he might settle a small annuity on the mother of Allegra, since Claire was 'now destitute of the means of subsistence; chiefly in consequence of the unfortunate circumstance which permits the tongue of malice to join her humble name with one of high celebrity'.[42] She wrote politely, but she considered it a 'claim not of charity but of justice', echoing the words of Mary Wollstonecraft: 'It is justice, not charity, that is wanting in the world.'[43] Byron refused, and rudely. At this Mrs Mason wrote to Mary Shelley, 'I will read no more of his poetry, for I shall always think of him as "a counterfeit & no true man" – He may roll in riches & get drunk with fame, but he will never be happy.'[44]

Claire had to fend for herself; she went as far afield as

Russia to work as a governess. Mary took her son to England. She refused to hand him over to Shelley's father, and was allowed only a pittance; so she wrote to occupy her mind, but also to make a living. The death of Shelley's son Charles in 1826 made Percy heir to the baronetcy, but he did not inherit until 1844, when both Mary and Claire benefited from Shelley's will at last.

Byron went his way to Greece, and died at Missolonghi in April 1824. On hearing of his death, Mrs Mason wrote to Mary Shelley, 'Your account of Lord B's sufferings make me pity him . . . Do you remember my last letter to Lord B. & what I said of "the sleepless bed of pain"? It appears to have been prophetic.' She added, 'I regret having written it, as it was to no purpose – but my motive was good.'[45]

IX

Respectability overtook Mrs Mason at last in 1826, when she married Tighe, three years after the death of Mountcashell; but, since the girls remained illegitimate, their mother remained suspicious of English prudery. 'For many reasons I have made it a rule to receive no English,' she wrote to Mary in 1827, adding that 'Nerina is quite an Italian . . . indeed so is Laurette also.'[46] Marriage did not improve relations between Tighe and his consort. He disapproved of the way in which she took the girls out into Pisan society and accused her of spending all her money without consulting him. She took little notice of these complaints, continuing serenely along her own course, and they occupied separate houses for much of the time, lunching *en famille* on Sundays, when she would have 'a respectable plumb pudding' ready for him.[47] The girls loved him and adored her.

She set an impressive example to them, keeping up her medical work among the poor; a shelf of books witnessed to her success as a writer, not only *Old Daniel* but *Advice to Young Mothers* 'by a Grandmother' (1823), which was translated into several languages. Her novel *The Sisters of Nansfield* was also published in England in 1824 and translated into Italian; she had no great opinion of it herself, and her story of two sisters in a country village, complete with curate and silly old ladies, reads like Jane Austen drained of everything that makes her worth reading. More brilliantly, she organized a literary society in 1827, the Accademia dei Lunatici, of which she was president and Laurette secretary. Members had to swear they were lunatics on joining, and they read humorous papers and poems. Most were young men from the university; the whimsicality may have provided a cover for political interests at a time when Tuscany was ruled by an Austrian archduke; many of the members went on to take part in the struggle for a united Italy.

When Claire arrived back in Pisa in 1831, the Accademia dei Lunatici was still going, but did not last much longer. Claire was invited to live with the family. 'Nothing can equal Mrs Mason's kindness to me. Hers is the only house except my mother's, in which all my life I have ever felt at home. With her I am as her child,' she wrote to Mary.[48] Although Mrs Mason pressed money on her, Claire promptly passed it on to Mary, and earned her own living as a daily governess in an English family. She also resumed the role of elder sister to Laurette and Nerina; the great topic had become Laurette's wish to marry a man everyone else considered disastrously unsuitable. Laurette's portrait, done at this time, shows her with dark hair in a great elaborate pile on top of her head, low-cut dress, tightly belted waist and huge puff sleeves. Her eyes were blue like her mother's, and she was much admired.

Adolphe Dominique Galloni d'Istria, the man so keen to marry her, claimed to be a prince, but his file in the French diplomatic archives makes it clear he was not.[49] His father was an infantry officer in Corsica, and young Galloni entered the French consular service in 1830 through the patronage of a Count Pozzo di Borgo. He was 'sujet à de violentes colères', according to his employers, and wooed Laurette with passion and, in Mary's account, 'at the dagger's point'.[50] He got himself posted to Genoa in 1831 with the plea that he was hoping to marry into a family resident in Italy, and he was determined to succeed. Laurette's parents were united in their horror at the prospect of such a husband. Tighe wrote to her objecting to the proposed marriage, 'of which I was casually informed as a circumstance likely to take place, without the slightest reference to my wishes or opinions', and continued, 'I now beg leave to repeat that nobody in their senses could properly give their consent to such a marriage.'[51] Mrs Mason also 'tried every means to hinder it', according to Claire. 'She cannot disguise her dislike of Galloni – he having nearly killed her with his scenes . . . It is the first time the mother and daughter were ever divided in opinion.'[52] Nerina hated Galloni too, foresaw a cruel fate for her sister, and declared that patriotism was a better cause for women than matrimony. She poured out her thoughts to Claire, after which the two of them would laugh 'at the ridiculous figures human beings cut in struggling all their might and main against a destiny which forces millions and millions of enormous planets on their way and against which all struggling is useless'.[53]

Claire described Galloni at various times as a beast, and as having 'vulgarity of the senses very strongly marked in his countenance, and strong passions'; but Laurette was set on the marriage, and it took place in November 1832.[54] In Claire's account again, the bride came home shortly after the wedding 'pale worn and sad' and took to her bed for three weeks. Then she returned to Genoa and insisted she was happy, 'but as she would not confess it, were it otherwise, we have doubts on the subject'.[55] In the autumn of 1833 Claire mentioned that 'Laurette is in the family way – to Mrs M's horror'; if she was, she lost the baby.[56]

Nerina's marriage was the happy one, in 1834, to one of the Lunatici, Bartolomeo Cini, 'the best & most delightful Pistoian' in Mary's words.[57] The Cinis were an old land-owning family, able and respected; Nerina's father-in-law set up a paper mill in San Marcello, providing jobs for the people as well as profits for the family. Mrs Mason approved thoroughly; but her health was failing, and she lived only to see Nerina's first child born. She died in January 1835 and was buried in the Protestant cemetery at Livorno. Neither her married name of Tighe nor her chosen name of Mrs Mason was on the gravestone, which read 'Margaret Jane Countess of Mount Cashell'. Tighe must have decided it was after all the most appropriate form for his consort of thirty years.

Nerina had become a Catholic on marrying; Laurette was an atheist, as Claire explained to Mary, complaining that she was expected to console Laurette for the loss of her mother by insisting on the immortality of the soul, which she did not believe in herself. She pitied Laurette's grief, the more so since 'it is now clear to every body, she does not love her husband one particle'.[58]

Glimpses of Laurette's life and opinions appear in the letters she wrote her father in the last two years of his life – he survived his wife for only that long. At first she followed Galloni wherever his consular appointments took him, and, when he was sent to Majorca in 1836, they travelled by way of Barcelona, arriving in mid-revolution; Laura described the city illuminated after the shooting of the Governor-General, and watched from her hotel window as his body was dragged through the streets to be burnt, to shouts of triumph from the people. The next day troops were brought in, and the Gallonis set sail for Palma. She detested Majorca and its people, finding the nobility profligate and the rest vulgar, and shut herself indoors: 'I retrench myself in my fortress,' she wrote.[59] 'I lead a sort of school girls life having set myself a task for almost every hour.'[60] The tasks were learning Spanish and reading Roman history; she also read Byron, Shakespeare, Dante and, as soon as her Spanish was good enough, Cervantes. Her programme reminds you of Mary Shelley's reading habits; but in the evenings Laurette's husband taught her to shoot, and she boasted that she rarely missed 'the circumference of an orange at a distance of 95 paces'.[61] It seems to have been the one thing she enjoyed doing with him.

In January 1836 she had a visit from 'the only person I have liked for six months'.[62] This was Captain Henry Codrington, in command of the *Orestes*, which put in at Palma. He was a six-foot-tall son of an admiral and a future admiral himself; he was also musical and blessed with a fine voice, and he and Laurette were soon singing duets at the piano and confiding to one another how much they detested garlic and bad oils, and longed for good potatoes. 'I have not yet myself learned to enjoy the charms of garlick or to smoke a Cigar,' she confessed. The Gallonis were invited to dine aboard the *Orestes*, and the weather being rough Laurette had to lie down on a sofa, 'which rather shocked me before an Englishman'.[63] Did she mean her bad sea legs, or the indecorum of lying down? Codrington liked her well enough to call again and sing some last duets before sailing on. It is a charming encounter between the gallant officer in William IV's navy and the blue-eyed beauty stranded in Majorca, ill married to a Corsican. She had hardly met an Englishman in her life, and he was not to know that Madame Galloni was the daughter of an Irish countess: or perhaps she told him. You want to hear more.

Majorca was a short posting. Galloni had no money, only debts; they were living on his small salary and £100 a year from her father, and Galloni pestered her to ask for more. She had to pass on her father's explanations that he had nothing left but his pension. After a while she wrote to him, 'you must forgive me if I decline entering further into money matters . . . While unmarried a woman has of course nothing to do with such affairs; once married, as you know, the husband takes the fortune great or small into his hands, and acts with it according as he thinks best; so that a wife has as little to do with money matters after, as before, marriage. So much I think it necessary to say in my own defence – not to pass for a complete fool.'[64] Since her husband was beyond control, her father was given the benefit of her crisp summary of the evils of the position of women, with its echo of Mary Wollstonecraft.

Galloni was offered another temporary posting at Civitavecchia. Laurette found the situation on the Italian coast near Rome agreeable; there was no company, and nothing to do but bathe, read and write letters, she said. This was in August 1836, and the records show that Galloni was replacing the regular consul, Henri Beyle, otherwise known as Stendhal. A few years before Mary had refused to review his book on Rome: 'M. Beyle's book is so trite so unentertaining – so *very* common place that I have found it quite impossible to do anything with it.'[65] It is a pity he and Laurette did not come face to face, since he was an admirer of beautiful women, an Anglophile and a man who knew a good deal about unhappiness in love; but he had taken leave to work on his Italian novel, *La Chartreuse de Parme*. It was published in 1839, a marvellous, complex book that moves from the battlefield of Waterloo to the political and amorous intrigues of life at an Italian court in the 1820s; there are extraordinary prison scenes, and the hero is driven to kidnap his own young son, who then falls ill and dies. It is one of the great novels of the nineteenth century; and if Galloni did nothing else good in his life, at least his taking over of Monsieur Beyle's tedious consular duties allowed him to concentrate on finishing *La Chartreuse de Parme*.

Laurette was beginning to think of attempting fiction herself. She was glad to be childless; what she had seen of the trials and tribulations of motherhood would not have encouraged her. 'Every day I thank my evil stars for this one good turn they have done me in life, leaving me without children,' she wrote to her father.[66] She worried about Nerina's babies; some of them flourished, but half of them died, and Nerina, once so blooming, was losing her health. Laurette wrote to her father again, 'I am afraid dearest Tatty I have little confidence left me in the good things of this world.'[67] She wrote this from Rome, and was there when her father died. Then her husband's work took him to Perugia, to Crete for two years, to Sardinia and in 1839 to Venice.

*

Laurette kept in touch with Claire, who was away from Italy, working in England, France and Germany during the 1840s, and with Mary in England. When Mary toured Italy in 1842/3 with her now adult son Percy, she spent enough time with Laurette to see that she was deeply unhappy in her marriage, and seemingly hopeless of any change for the better. 'Much as I abhor & shrink from a public life for women it would be better than the present state of things,' she wrote to a friend; and to Claire, 'she mourns over herself helplessly, bitterly'.[68] 'Unless one murdered Galloni & married her to a Prince I do not see how one could render her happier.'[69] Galloni was in Paris at this point, under investigation by the authorities for alleged mishandling of public money. Claire, also in Paris, observed him living 'in the first style'. 'Poor Laura – what had you ever done to deserve so hard a fate?' she asked.[70]

Glad as Mary was to see Laurette, she found her chilly; but it may have been discretion rather than a cold heart that made her guarded. There was something she may not have told Mary: the existence of a Sicilian admirer. In truth she was in Sicily for considerable periods from 1843 until 1847. Her admirer was Placido Tardy, a mathematician, a few years younger than her; he was everything Galloni was not, highly intelligent, disinterested, politically congenial and devoted to her. Galloni's acquittal in 1844 did not restore his wife to him. A French police report of 1848 said he was married to an Italian 'issue de parents riches' but had spent all her money and run up debts; and in 1849 he was sent to Moscow. Claire decided he was to be a spy there, and was very likely right. By then Laurette was living more or less openly with Tardy, who left Sicily after the uprising of 1847 and moved to Florence. The Cinis approved and welcomed them to San Marcello: and they were sharing lodgings in Florence in the summer of 1849.

Now Laurette in her turn became a writer. She wrote to Mary asking for help and advice about becoming a novelist, and when her first attempt, *Inez de Medine*, was published in Naples in 1846, Mary offered to help her find an English publisher. Mary also wrote to a friend, 'I hope & trust, highly gifted as she is – that her work will be such as to bear the impress of her intellect – If it does! How a million times delighted I shall be – It may happen with all her talents she may want a something – & her productions may fail . . . so till one has seen the work highly as I think of Laura, I know it is a lottery.'[71] Mary was right to be cautious. She began to translate *Inez*. Two chapters among her papers in the Bodleian must have been enough to dismay her, and her translation falls into every cliché, including the famous 'vortex of dissipation' against which Jane Austen warned. A Don Juan abducts Inez, who is rescued by the French navy; in Barcelona, Don Juan's sister Dolores lures Inez's brother into 'a very vortex of pleasure and dissipation', while Inez goes mad in Paris. *Inez* did not appear in English, and nothing more was heard of it, or of its successor, *Dolore e Vendetta*.

Laurette was never published in England; she lost her only hope when Mary died in 1851. But in other ways her life took a dramatic turn for the better. In 1852 Galloni was appointed to Puerto Rico. By now Tardy had been given a chair at Genoa by Cavour; and when news came of Galloni's death early the following year, of 'gout of the stomach and brain', Laurette and Tardy were at last able to marry. Happy and settled, she took up her writing again, using the pseudonym of 'Sara'. Dismissing her early books as apprentice work, she described *Una Madre* as her first novel in 1857. It is dedicated to her mother's memory, and pays tribute to Countess Mountcashell in the character of a good Venetian Countess Melin, who visits the poor, provides them with medical advice, cares nothing for fashion or appearances, and gives exceptional love and support to her two daughters; sadly, she is otherwise not much like Lady Mountcashell. Laurette Tardy still held to the belief that fiction required melodrama: the Countess is kept busy preserving both her married daughters from the same vile seducer, and is driven to attack him with a knife when one daughter kills herself in despair after giving birth to his child. All this is played out against the Venetian rising of 1848, in which the Countess's younger son loses his life fighting the Austrians; the elder son has chosen to live in England and dissipated the family fortune gambling, leaving his mother to make ends meet by letting out their palazzo on the Grand Canal to wealthy foreigners. So it goes on, the brew too rich, the characters too thin.

In another story she adds Gothic elements to the theme of marital villainy: a Sardinian count, acting at the behest of his mistress, hires an assassin to kill his young wife in their remote mountain castle. The wife is wounded, and when she recovers she flees Sardinia with her child and faithful maid. They are shipwrecked, arrive penniless in France and settle in a peasant house near Nîmes. A mysterious hermit in a black hood is seen in the neighbourhood, and arrives just in time to save them from a band of rioting socialists. He turns out to be the suitor she had rejected for the evil count, who opportunely dies, leaving them free to marry. Had Laurette only written from her own experience, she might well have produced something more interesting.

The story of Sardinia and the French socialists was published with a collection of essays reprinted from newspapers and magazines, women's themes alternating with essays on Democracy, Conscience, the importance of Truth-telling: they are decent but not exceptional. At least they testify to her capacity for hard work; four volumes of them were published in Milan in 1868 under the title *La Spettatrice* – a reminder of the old volumes of *The Spectator* in her parents' library.

Before starting to read Laurette Tardy's work I hoped she might turn out to be an Italian George Eliot. I was wildly off the mark. But she did address herself to the situation of women, and not just women of the upper classes; there are servants and actresses as well as countesses in her stories. She also took an interest in the politics of her country during the years of the Risorgimento. She was clearly an intelligent woman; she simply did not light on a form that allowed her to say anything original, or a living voice for her characters. Her letters, written in English, have twice the life of her Italian fiction. Perhaps she should have written in English. Finding copies of her novels proved so difficult that I have not seen them all, and there may yet be a jewel I have missed. I can't help hoping so, not least because Laurette is the intellectual grandchild of Mary Wollstonecraft as well as the friend of Mary Shelley.

Laurette and Nerina kept up their friendships with Mary and Claire. Claire returned to Tuscany in 1859 and lived the last twenty years of her life there, in close contact with the Cinis. They had become her family, the most stable point in her long and difficult life: 'Laura, Nerina and Cini are from now onwards (with the exception of my little nephew [she meant Percy]) the beings most dear to me in the whole world,' she wrote after the death of Mrs Mason.[72] She asked Bartolomeo Cini to be her executor, and, although she outlived both him and Nerina, one of her last letters is to their daughter Margherita, asking for news of Laurette.

Claire died in 1879, Laurette only a year after her. Upon her death Tardy left Genoa and moved to San Marcello, welcomed by Nerina and Bartolomeo's son, Giovanni Cosimo Cini. The house was so big that Tardy was able to take all Laurette's possessions with him, and stack them away out of sight; among them was the manuscript of Mary's *Maurice*. There it remained, and there he remained too, a neat white-bearded figure, wearing a white suit in the San Marcello photograph albums, watching the next generation grow up, and then the next; and frightening little Giovanna with his beard. When he died in 1914 there were other things to think about than going through his boxes; and after the First World War came political upheavals, another war, losses and tragedies in the family. Even when American scholars and collectors arrived in the 1950s and 1960s, Laurette's boxes remained undisturbed. Then Casa Cini was divided, a whole wing sold and turned into offices and flats; in clearing that wing, Laurette's boxes were moved to the library. So it was that only in 1997, exactly two hundred years after Mary Shelley's birth, was her story brought to light by Cristina Dazzi, the wife of Lady Mountcashell's great-great-great-grandson.

NOTE ON THE TEXT

The text of *Maurice* appears twice in this edition. The first version is corrected and slightly modernized for ease of reading. The second shows Mary Shelley's original lineation, pagination, spelling, punctuation, corrections and emendations; only the old double 's' has been modernized. The manuscript has been re-set line for line, with vertical rules indicating the original page breaks.

MAURICE,
or the Fisher's Cot

For Laurette from her friend Mrs Shelley

Maurice,
or the
Fisher's Cot

A Tale

PART I

One Sunday afternoon in the month of September, a traveller entered the town of Torquay, a seaport on the southern coast of Devonshire. The afternoon was pleasant and warm, and the waves of the sea, slightly agitated by a breeze, sparkled under the sun. The streets of the town were empty, for the inhabitants after having been to church were dining during the interval between the services: so the traveller walked on through the meaner streets of the town, to the semicircle of houses that surrounds the harbour; and then he paused at the door of a neat-looking inn. The traveller was a man about forty-five years of age; he was remarkably erect in his person; alert and even graceful in his walk; his hair was black and curly, although a little fallen from his temples; he was handsome, but somewhat sun-burnt, and when he smiled he looked so good-tempered and kind that you could not see him without loving him. In dress and manner he had the appearance of one who had seen better days, but who was now poor; and he seemed serious, though not depressed by poverty. His clothes were coarse and covered with dust; he was on foot, and had a wallet* buckled on his back.

He entered the inn, and asking for dinner, unbuckled his wallet, and sat down to rest himself near the door. While he was thus sitting a funeral passed by: it was evidently the funeral of a poor person; the coffin was carried by some peasants, and four mourners followed. Three of these, although serious, looked careless and indifferent; the fourth was a boy of about thirteen years of age; he was crying, and was so much taken up by his own distress that he did not observe anything that passed near him. Something in this boy's appearance attracted the traveller's attention; and once, when he ceased crying and looked round towards the inn door, the traveller thought that he had seldom seen so beautiful a youth. He turned to the landlady, and asked, whose was that funeral? And who was the boy that accompanied it?

"That," replied the woman, "is the funeral of old Barnet, the fisherman: and that boy was a kind of servant or apprentice who lived with him after the death of the old dame, his wife."—

* *wallet* in the old sense of a traveller's bag or knapsack.

"Does he belong to this town?"—

"He does not; nor do I know from whence he comes: he is the child of poor people or his parents would never have sent him to live in the cottage of old Barnet. The neighbours says he is a good boy, but I know nothing about him."

The traveller sighed and said: "This poor boy can be nothing to me, yet I am much pleased with his appearance and manner."—A young countryman who was dining at a table in a corner of the room now rose, and said: "I live near old Barnet's cottage, and know this boy well; he is the best creature in the world, and all who know him love him: as you, sir, appear inquisitive about him, I will, if you please, relate all I know concerning him."—The traveller expressed his assent and the countryman began thus:—

"Old Barnet's cottage is situated about three miles from this town at the foot of the cliff and overhung by a few trees; it is very solitary and very poor; the spring tide comes up almost to the steps of the door; and when the wind blows the spray of the sea is dashed against the windows. We neighbours often wondered how so old a cot could stand the stress of weather; or being so near the sea that some high south winds do not blow the waves entirely over it; but it is sheltered by the crag, and being built on ground somewhat higher than the shore, out of the reach of the most tempestuous waves, it stands there, as I have known it stand ever since I was born, an old weather-beaten cot, the roof covered with lichens and moss. Beside it is a little cove where the fishing boat is kept, and there is an outhouse where the nets and sails were placed when the old man returned from the sea. A little freshwater brook trickles from the cliff, close to it, down into the sea, and when I was a boy I used often to go and place paper boats in this rill and watch them sailing down to the sea where they were soon lost in the great waves.*

"Old Barnet and his dame lived here. He was a most hard-working old man; early and late you saw his little skiff at sea, and often when no other boats ventured out Barnet would go and come back with fine, fresh fish for the Torquay market. His dame was so lame that she seldom moved from the old, worsted, high-backed armchair where she used to sit mending the nets, and hearing a few children read, who came to her from the neighbouring farmhouses. Our farm is only half a mile distant from the cot and I am one of those who learned to read in Dame Barnet's great Bible. She would not be paid for this, calling it merely a good neighbourly turn; but every Sunday I used to bring her a basket of vegetables and fruits, and every autumn she had a dozen of our best cider.

"Well about a year ago this good woman died, and all the children about wept at her funeral: for besides hearing them read, which she always did without scolding them (her only punishment was not allowing us to visit her), she would make nice worsted balls for them and tell them stories of Goody Two-shoes and the Babes in the Wood, or sing to them the ballad of Chevy Chase and many

* Sailing paper boats was a favourite sport of Shelley's.

others which pleased us who were older as well as the children.* Besides she would do them a thousand services of mending their clothes when torn by accident and a thousand other little services which made her a great favourite with all. Barnet was very much grieved when she died: she was of little help to him not being able to move from her armchair without great difficulty; but when he came home wet from fishing, during the stormy winter days when every wave almost broke over his boat, she would contrive to have the fire lighted for him and the little old cottage set in order for his supper. But after her death when he returned from sea he was obliged to go hungry and sometimes dripping wet to the market at this town; and when he returned he was not handy at cooking his food or cleaning his room: besides he was now obliged to mend his nets for himself, and that took up a great deal of his time so that he did not catch so much fish as before. All these things made him melancholy; and he came about two months after his dame's death to our farm with tears

* *Goody Two-shoes* is a moralistic children's story, believed to be by Oliver Goldsmith (1730–74). 'The Babes in the Wood' is a ballad telling the story of a brother and sister whose uncle plans to murder them and hires killers who take them to a wood. One repents and kills the other, but then abandons the children, and they die of exposure and hunger in the wood, where the birds cover their bodies with leaves. It was already old when T. Percy printed it in his *Reliques of Ancient English Poetry* (1765). 'Chevy Chase' is also a very early and popular ballad in which the English Earl of Northumberland, Percy, decides to hunt over the land of his Scottish neighbour, Earl Douglas, without asking leave. A fight follows, and both lords are killed.

in his eyes, and said he thought he should give up his fishing and go up the country to seek his fortune, for that the old cottage under the cliff had become quite hateful to him since his dame's death. He was a hale old man, but his hair was as white as snow, and his back bent with age, so that it was a piteous thing to hear him talk of leaving his cot, and his boat, and all that he had in the world to seek his fortune among strangers. My father comforted him, and made him dine with us, and promised to send my sister Betsy sometimes to put his cottage in order: so he went home with a lighter heart than he came.

"The next day the wind blew into shore, and the old man, not being able to go out with his boat, sat down on a piece of rock that formed a kind of seat near his cot, and began to mend his nets. While he was thus employed this same boy of whom we speak, whose name is Maurice, came and sat down on the rock near him. The boy was a stranger in this part of the country, so after having saluted one another they both remained silent for some time; at length Maurice said:—'I think I could help you in that work and as I have nothing to do I wish you would let me try.'—

"'Try, and welcome,' said Barnet; 'but how is it that you have nothing to do? Good boys ought to work; you do not belong to these parts, and it is not well to see a boy of your age wandering about the country alone.'—'My parents are poor,' replied Maurice, 'and not being able to maintain me, I have tried to earn my own livelihood; I have been brought up to no trade, and have always been weakly and unable to work hard. When I left home I came with a man I knew to a farm not far distant, where they gave me work in plenty in the fields, the stables and the barns. I worked hard, for my master was severe, so at length I fell ill; then when I could work no longer they turned me away, and I think I should have died had not a poor woman taken care of me. She was so poor that I would not be a burden to her any longer than was necessary, and now I am too weak to work for my old master, so I am thrown on the wide world, and would be much obliged to anyone who would help me either by giving me such work as I can do, or advising me where I can go to get it; for I am willing, and although I say it myself, I am honest and have always been considered handy and industrious.'

"Old Barnet looked up in the boy's face; you know how pretty a lad he is; he was then sickly-looking and that made him a fitter object for compassion: he has the sweetest voice in the world and all that he said seemed to go to the old man's heart. He thought:—I have no child upon earth: my only relation is a brother who disdains a poor old fisherman like me. My dame is dead, and I am alone without anyone to help me if I am sick or to say a cheerful, 'Goodbye, God send you luck!' when I go a fishing. Surely this boy seems sent by heaven to me, and it seems to me that I love him already as if he were my own son. He shall stay with me; I can maintain him as I maintained my poor wife who is gone: he can put my cottage in order, mend my sails and nets, and on windy evenings who knows but he may be able to read the Bible to me as my dame used.'

"This was a lucky thought; the bargain was soon struck, and ever since Maurice has lived with old Barnet in his cottage. He is a good boy, honest, handy and clever: when we came to know him all our house loved him; he is able to read very tolerably, so my little brothers went to him to learn every Sunday as they used to go to the Dame, and no one can be more good-tempered. He made the old cottage quite another thing, cleaning it, and mending the old chairs; whitewashing the grate, and furbishing up the pans and saucepans; and laying them in neat rows. He was always merry, always at work, always ready to do a good turn for the poor as well as the rich. Old Barnet loved him better and better, and often thanked God for the day when he first came to the cottage. Out at sea the old man saw through the day the trees wave over his cottage roof, and at night he could distinguish the candle which Maurice placed at the window to direct him where to steer. When he came to shore the boy was always waiting there to help him draw his boat up to the cove. Then in winter he found a nice fire ready to dress his supper, and the table spread with a coarse, old, but clean cloth. In the morning when he went to market, Maurice heaved the water out of his boat, mended his nets, put his sails in order, and said a smiling, 'God give you luck!' when he went to sea. They lived several months in this manner very happily, and now a week ago old Barnet died."—

The countryman paused, and the traveller asked, "What

will become of the boy?"—"I do not know; but he is so much loved that I do not think he will come to want. For my part I am now leaving the country for a few weeks, for I am going to visit my grandmother who lives at Sidmouth; but when I return the first question I shall ask is what is become of Maurice. I have told you a long story, sir, but I hope you will excuse me; you have now finished your dinner, and I will detain you no longer. Good-bye!"—"Thank you heartily. Good-day, and a pleasant journey to you," was the reply, and the young man left the inn.

The traveller remained some time leaning his head on his hand, thinking what he should do. He wanted very much to make further enquiry about Maurice, but when he thought of the business he had at Exeter he could not resolve to delay his journey: so after resting himself another hour, he strapped on his wallet and left the inn, following the Exeter road.

The next morning he arrived at this city. By and by I shall explain what his business there was; but at present I shall only say that having passed three anxious days, he was obliged to give up his business, and to determine to return whence he came, that he might enquire whether something had not happened in the mean time that might help him; at the same time he resolved on his way back to visit old Barnet's cottage, and to enquire what had become of Maurice, and to offer his services in placing him in some suitable situation, where he might honestly get his livelihood without being worked too hard. And now leaving him to walk with his wallet on his back along the road which leads from Exeter to Torquay, let us take a peep into the cottage under the cliff; and see what has become of Maurice and what help he is likely to get in his misfortunes.

PART SECOND

The three other mourners who had followed Old Barnet's funeral were the brother of whom the countryman had spoken, and his two sons. After the funeral this brother, who was a shopkeeper at Torquay and a money-loving man, spoke thus to Maurice:—"You, it seems, were maintained by my poor brother, and lived in his cottage: now you know by the laws that since my brother died without a will, all he was worth, the cottage and its furniture, the boat and his nets are mine. If they were not, you are too young to follow his trade, so there is no possible reason why you should remain in the cottage. The neighbours say you are an honest lad so I would not be too hard upon you; you may stay in the cottage one week, and you can employ yourself in seeking for a place: at the end of that time a friend of mine with his three sons will come and live there, and having bought the boat will carry on the fishing; they will not want you for a servant, so by that time you must remove. You are honest and therefore I need hardly tell you that nothing in the cottage belongs to you, except what you brought yourself, and that you will not be allowed to take anything away with you."—

Maurice thanked his old friend's brother for allowing him to stay a week in the cottage; he intended to have asked his advice about what he ought to do, but there was something so dry and forbidding in his manner that he could not make up his mind to speak, but went away, walking sorrowfully along the shore towards the old cottage. When he arrived he thought that it looked so desolate and strange, that he had not the heart to enter but sat down near the little freshwater brook, and watched the waves of the sea breaking at his feet. For the first time for several months he was idle; for it was no use to mend the nets when his old protector could not use them, or to get supper ready when he felt his heart too full to eat. He cried for the loss of his dear Barnet till he was quite tired, and then watched the sun set in the blue sea; and half imagined that perhaps Barnet was not dead, but out fishing and that he could perceive his white sail far out at sea: but turning round he saw the boat lying empty in the cove, and then he knew it must be true that his only friend was dead, and that he was now alone in the world. At length quite exhausted by sorrow, and feeling cold as the evening breeze arose and whitened the sea with foam, he got up and opening the cottage door, without eating any supper or striking a light, he knelt down and said his prayers and then went to bed.

Several days passed in this manner, and at length he began to think that he ought not to live this idle life any longer. The week was almost gone when he must quit the cottage, and then what should he do to earn bread to eat? Sometimes he thought he would return to his parents, but that he quickly determined not to do; and at length he resolved to go to farmer Benson, the father of the countryman who related his story to the traveller at Torquay. As he determined this he sat on his accustomed stone near the freshwater rill, and looked at the ocean which was unbroken by waves, and the sky where the sun had set, and the evening star gleamed in the golden light he had left behind him: the air was quite calm and the murmuring of the tide, which was going out, just broke the silence, while a few seagulls flew to their nests in the cliff over his head. Maurice heard a step near him, and turning round saw approach a kind, good-looking man who was indeed the traveller whom I described at the beginning of my story. The boy was much surprised, for a stranger had never before visited the cottage, which was two miles from any road: rising with his usual good nature, he asked him whether he had lost his way, and offered to show him the way to the nearest town.

"I have not lost my way," said the traveller, "I came to this cottage on purpose. I have particular reasons for wishing to see it, and would be much obliged to you if you could afford me a bed tonight."—"You are very welcome; the cottage is poor, but as the bed is clean perhaps you will be content."—"I have travelled too much, my good boy, not to be easily satisfied. But do not rise; for the present let us enjoy this pleasant evening here at the seaside, watching the waves that leave so smooth a beach behind them. Your cottage is built in a very pretty place."—"I think so indeed, and although it is poor and very old, yet taking it altogether I do not think there is a prettier in all the country round. The trees fall over and shelter it, a number of pretty flowers grow beside the brook which comes running down from the tall, red cliff. And nothing to my mind can be more beautiful than the moss and lichens, yellow, green, white and blue, that grow on the old thatched roof, making it look finer than a slated roof could possibly be. In the spring yellow wallflowers grow there, and the green before the door is covered with daisies. Besides if you come round to the other side where the cottage faces the hill you will find a pretty lattice grown over with honeysuckles and several geraniums in a stand outside the window. The geraniums were the great favourite of old Barnet's dame, and he loved them for her sake. Mr Gregory Barnet says that I must take nothing from the cottage, and that I know very well; but if farmer Benson will take me into his service I will spend two shillings that I have in buying the geraniums, if the man who is coming to live here will be kind enough to sell them."—"You intend then to leave this cottage?"—"I must. I am not strong enough to manage the boat and go out to sea, and so it is let to some fisherman; next Sunday I go away; but I hope I shall get work hereabouts, and I do not think I shall be unhappy, for I have seldom cried about my own misfortunes when I have been very ill-used indeed; and I do not dislike work when it does not make me ill. I loved old Barnet and liked my life here with him and I cried very much when he died—but if I can get work about a farmyard, I hope in a month or two to sing as cheerfully as I used when I saw his white sail among the other boats which you see out at sea."

Maurice did not say all this at once, but the stranger smiled so kindly, and asked so many questions in so affectionate a manner, that the boy was easily induced to open his whole heart to him, and to talk about his affairs as to an old friend. "I shall not return to my parents," said he, "for I left determining never more to see them till I could earn my own bread. My father works hard and wages are low, so being hardly able to get sufficient food for himself he was angry that he had to maintain an idle boy, and my mother is sufficiently vexed by him without my misfortunes being added to her cares. Unfortunately I am a delicate boy and unable to work as he would have me and have often been confined to my bed with fevers. My father never would believe I was really ill and would beat me and send me to bed without my supper when I could hardly stand. I do not mean to complain of him, and though I have told all this to you who are so kind, pray do not mention it to anyone else."

Thus they chatted till the evening star had set, and the sea became invisible through darkness, except indeed the white heads of the waves that broke near them; for the tide was coming in and the rock on which they sat began to be wetted by the spray: so they entered the cottage and supping on bread and salad, they presently after went to bed, the traveller telling the boy that he would both breakfast and dine with him the following day.

Maurice awoke before light, and leaving his guest sleeping soundly in bed he ran as fast as he could to Torquay to buy some white bread, and potatoes and meat for their breakfast and dinner. He was obliged to spend for this provision the two shillings with which he had intended to purchase his dear geraniums, and this made him a little sorrowful: but he was a cheerful, happy-tempered boy, and consoled himself with thinking that he would work doubly hard to earn this money before the next spring, and that he would entreat the future tenant of the cottage to take care of these pretty shrubs until that time.

When he arrived at the cottage he found the traveller seated on the rock on the beach; they greeted one another kindly, and Maurice, at the request of his guest, brought out a little table on the sands, and placed their breakfast on it in the open air; for it was a fine warm morning without a cloud in the sky. Their breakfast was plain and countrified, consisting of bread, a piece of cheese and a basin of that nice clouted cream that they make in Devonshire;* and our two friends ate so heartily of what was there that very little remained. They then continued sitting on the rock talking of the pleasure of living in the country, of seeing the pretty flowers grow in the hedges and among the green grass; of the beauty of the little birds, and the cruelty of those who kill them: and the sweet life it would be to take care of a nice farm, not working too hard, but sufficient to become healthy and strong through exercise; and in the evening to read entertaining books, telling them of how the earth is cultivated, and how various

* *clouted cream*, now known as clotted cream.

countries bring forth various fruits: of the sea, and how different voyages and discoveries have been made on it: of the sky, and how the beautiful stars which we see at night move, and the signs they make of winter and summer. The traveller told Maurice that there were books more delightful than these which told of what good and wise men had done a great many years ago; how some had died to serve their fellow creatures, and how through the exertions of these men everyone had become better, wiser and happier. Maurice said that he had never read any book of that kind except the Bible, and that he had often cried over the distress of Joseph, when he was sold to slavery, and over the sorrow of David, when his son Absalom revolted against him.

At length, after a pause, the traveller said:—"You talk, my dear Maurice, of going to seek for work at farmer Benson's: now what say you if instead of this, you came and lived with me. I would not task you too hard, but would give you some of these pretty books to read, and would do my best to make you happy."—Maurice looked up at the kind stranger and saw him smiling benevolently after him. "How good you are!"—he replied.—"I will be good to you," said his guest, "but I am a stranger and you may be afraid to go away with one whom you never saw before. It is late now for we have talked a long time, so let us go in and prepare our dinner, and afterwards we will come and sit here again and I will tell you who I am; why I am travelling on foot about the country; what my disappointments have been, and what my hopes are."—

They did as he said. They made a good fire and placed their meat and potatoes to boil. Maurice filled a jug with clear water from the brook, and the traveller took a small bottle of good wine from his wallet. By noon the dinner was ready, and after they had finished they sat down on the rock, and the traveller began his relation.

PART THIRD

"I am the son of a professor of mathematics at the University of Oxford; my father was not rich but he gave me an excellent education, and I was exceedingly industrious and fond of learning. As long as I can remember I never went about without a book in my pocket, and loved to take long, solitary walks, and then to sit and read for hours together under the shade of trees, and beside the river; when I did not as an idler go to sleep, lulled by its murmuring, but I used to study and reflect with great earnestness and curiosity. Everything about me appeared wonderful to my eyes, and I wanted to know why the water of the river always ran and never became less; how the sun was governed as it passed along the sky, and why the moon changed as it did, and sometimes appeared round, and full, and yellow, and at other times only a little silver crescent. There was also another thing which delighted me extremely, which was to examine three large volumes of prints of beautiful ancient temples that my father possessed. I spent whole days in looking at these, and reading the accounts of their dimensions and how they were built; for I thought I should be the happiest creature in the world if ever I should be able to build such beautiful edifices as I saw represented in these books. As I grew older I became fonder and fonder of architecture, and as no knowledge is gained without application I passed my whole time in learning mathematics and those sciences which best teach us how to erect edifices such as the ancients used to build. When I was five and twenty my kind father sent me abroad to Asia, Italy and Greece to visit the remains of the old temples that still exist, and I passed five years in this happy manner, dwelling among foreign nations, often in desert places where the people do not live by sowing and reaping corn and taking care of farms, as they do here, but depend upon hunting for their livelihood, leaving their native villages for months together in search of game, and living a wild life among the woods and mountains, while their wives and daughters remain at home spinning their own clothes, sitting in the open air, where the winters are so mild that they have neither frost or snow.*

"When I returned to England I applied to business, and being a good architect I soon became rich. When I thought I had money enough I gave up my business and applied myself to country labours and all kinds of study, which I liked better than building churches and bridges where the people have too little taste or too little money to allow them to be built in the beautiful manner I wished.

"I married at this time a lady, whom you will soon see, my dear Maurice, and then you will know how wise and good she is. Soon after our marriage we had a little boy of whom we were dotingly fond. All our joy was in watching

---

* Mary Shelley is possibly drawing on Byron's accounts of his travels for the traveller's observations of life in Asia, Italy and Greece.

this little creature, who was as beautiful and good as it was possible to be. When he was two years old we made a journey during the summer and stayed for a month at Ilfracombe, a seaport more than fifty miles' distance from this place, and here a misfortune happened to us since which we have never been perfectly contented. It is now eleven years ago, but I can never think of that time without being unhappy.

"We used often to ride out, my wife and I, and a servant with our baby; and when we came to a pretty place we used to leave the nurse and child with the carriage while we took long walks in the country. One day we rode until we came to the banks of a very pretty river; and telling the nurse to wait for us, we walked on for several miles, enjoying the pleasant weather, listening to the singing of the birds in the elm trees which hung over the river, and watching the little insects with wings of purple, green and gold that flew on the surface of the water.

"When we returned we were dreadfully frightened to find the nurse asleep among some hay and no child near her. We awoke the woman and she became pale with fear and trembled all over when she found the child gone; since he had gone to sleep in her arms, and she, without thinking of the danger, and lulled to sleep by the sun, had at last fallen asleep also. The first thing we did was to run to the river;—but I will not describe to you, my little friend, the great grief we felt during this search. We did not find our child, or see any remains of him near the water; on the contrary we found one of his little shoes in a field about a mile from the river, and this made us think that perhaps he was stolen. We spent many months in searching the whole country, but in vain, we could not hear any tidings of our dear, lost boy.

"For my part I have never given up hope that I shall one day find him again, for I always felt convinced that he was not drowned. So every year I spend two months in Devonshire going over the whole county looking for him. I dress myself meanly that I may enter the cottages with greater freedom and make enquiries of the country people in a familiar manner; I walk about from village to village, and never pass a solitary cottage without looking at the children, and asking questions concerning them.

"A fortnight ago I passed by a cottage about five miles from Ilfracombe, at the door of which stood a woman crying and wringing her hands: I stopped and asked her what was the matter, and she told me that her husband had died two days before, and that her only son had been away a year and a half and she did not know what had become of him. I tried to console her, and told her that I also was unhappy and had lost my only child while a baby and had never found him again. I then related to her my misfortune and was much surprised to find her more distressed than before, and when I described to her the great grief of my wife, she cried out, 'I am the cause of this! I am the wicked woman who stole your child!' I started at these words, and as soon as I could speak I asked her what had become of my poor dear boy. She then began to cry again, and said that it was him she lamented when she told me that she had not seen her only son for nearly two years. She cried so much and appeared so distressed that I was obliged to spend almost an hour before I could console her, and then she told me how all had happened.

"Her husband had been a sailor and they had lived several years together and had had no children: he was a bad man, and would beat and reproach her for not having a child, which made her very unhappy, and she thought that she would be perfectly happy if heaven would bless her with a son. At length once when her husband went on a long voyage, she wrote to him a month after his departure and told him that she was with child. He stayed away a long time, and she continued to write and to tell falsehoods, how the child was born and was thriving; and she did this foolishly without thinking of the consequences, or what her husband would say when he returned and found no child. He was a sailor on board a king's ship, and getting a wound in a battle which disabled him for a long time he wrote to her who was then living in London, to go down to his native place at Ilfracombe, for that he would leave his ship and go and live there the rest of his days.

"She went down with a sorrowful heart, not knowing what she should say about her pretended child; and, not liking to go among his relations, who all expected to see a fine stout boy about two years old, she took a mean lodging in a town some miles off and went by a false name. She passed two months in a very unhappy state of mind, strolling about the country and not able to determine as to what she would do, when one day for our great misfortune she determined to walk towards Ilfracombe to find out whether her husband had arrived, and on her way she found our poor baby asleep in the arms of his careless nurse.

"One wicked thing brings on another; and she who had deceived her husband, and for two years written a number of falsehoods, and had come to have the habit of feeling guilty and wrong, now made up her mind to steal this child, not caring for the unhappiness of its parents. She took him gently out of the nurse's arms, and ran with him across the fields towards the town where she had been living for the last two months. When she came near the town she hid the child under some straw in a barn, and went as fast as she could to her lodgings. She paid for them and taking her bundle of clothes she went back to the child and hid herself in the barn all day. At night she began her journey. She resolved to go to Plymouth and wait for her husband, whose ship was expected in that port, and thus to quit the country near Ilfracombe until her theft should be forgotten. She walked all day and hid herself at night for fear of being discovered. She burned the child's good clothes and made it others out of her own, preserving only a little coral necklace with his Christian name engraved on the clasp and the remaining shoe, whose fellow we found in the field and which we have ever kept with great affection. She lived six months at Plymouth before her husband arrived and then they went together and settled themselves in the cottage where I found them. The woman soon loved our poor boy as if he had been her own and took all possible care of him—caressing and tending him with the tenderness of a mother.

"But people who do that which they ought not to do seldom find that good comes from the crimes they commit which they expect. Our poor boy had been accustomed to delicate fare and gentle nursing; and whether it was that he was now fed poorly and neglected (not through unkindness, but because she had not leisure to give him the attention to which he had been accustomed with us), whether it were on these accounts I know not, but our little Henry became sickly and delicate, and lost that fine bloom which first tempted her to the wicked action of stealing him. Her husband, who was a bad man and who had before grumbled that he had no child, now became more cross than ever, saying that the sickly brat would never come to good, and that he was obliged to maintain him by the sweat of his brow when he would never be able to do the like for him when he was old.

"The woman then said to me:—'I have been very miserable as well as wicked: for not only I felt great repentance at having taken this baby from his parents, but I found my husband unkinder than ever, and that instead of loving, he perfectly disliked the poor child. Besides the dear fellow lost his health and although the best creature in the world and the most willing and clever, yet he could do no hard work, and often had fevers and other illnesses when my husband grudged the doctor, and I used to sit crying by his bedside thinking that if his rich parents had still kept him he would not lie without help on his sickbed.

"'As he grew older my husband grew unkinder and sometimes beat him because he could not work, and treated him in so cruel a manner that I dare not relate to you who are his father, so one day Henry (for so I called him as by his broken words I found his parents had named him) came to me, and told me that farmer Jackson had promised to get work for him, and that he was determined to go and try if he could not gain his own livelihood. I cried bitterly, but could not alter his purpose, though then I would have given all I had in the world to find out who his rich parents were, that I might restore him. I gave him my blessing and he went away and I have never heard of him since!'

"I will not tire you, my little friend, with the account of my walks and anxieties for this last fortnight; during which I have been employed in going all over Devonshire tracing my lost child; my labours have been unsuccessful. I am now going to return to Dame Smithson to ask whether he has returned to her. This is my story; do you consent to come and live with me? If I never find my darling boy you shall be a son to me, and if I do find him——"

Maurice had listened to this relation very attentively, and near the end his eyes had streamed with tears and he showed every sign of interest and impatience: and now when the traveller said these words he threw himself into his arms and sobbed out—"I am your son! Daddy Smithson is not my father! I am your lost boy!"—And then he told him how he had always considered Dame Smithson his mother, and how kind to him and fond of him she was; and how her husband had made him perfectly miserable so that he had determined never to go home again until he should be able to earn his bread for himself. He said that he had called himself Maurice because he was afraid that the cruel man whom he thought his father might come to that part of the country and find him out and beat and ill-use him as he used to do at home.

Now nothing could be happier than the traveller and his dear son as they sat together by the seaside, talking about what they would do and the joy of his poor mother when she should see him again. Henry cried for joy when he thought of the happy life they should lead, reading delightful books, living with a kind father and mother, and having no care upon earth but that of obeying them and making them happy. They went that very evening to Torquay, and hiring a chaise they rode towards the traveller's home; and never rested until they arrived and Henry was in his mother's arms.

And what became of the old moss-roofed cottage by the seaside? Why, at Henry's request his father bought it, and the boat, and the geraniums, and all that belonged to it from Mr Gregory Barnet. They could not live there because Henry was obliged to go to Eton* to school; and

* Eton College, near Windsor, is England's foremost school for boys, founded by King Henry VI for sons of noblemen and scholars who traditionally went on to study at King's College, Cambridge. Eton was attended both by Shelley and by George Tighe, Laurette's father.

his father's house was near Windsor park, close to the school, so that he always lived with his dear parents. But in the Whitsuntide and Bartholomewtide holidays* they went down to Devonshire to visit the pretty cottage and lived in it two months every year. It was too small for any servants to come with them, so Henry put on a coarse country dress, and his father clothed himself as he used when he travelled about the country to seek for his child. They took care of the garden, bought their own food, cooked their own dinner; and when the weather was fine and the sun shone they sat on the rock near the freshwater rill and talked about all the beautiful things they had seen or would one day see, or read delightful books whose knowledge and lessons made them both wiser and happier. When they were at this cottage Henry always went by the name of Maurice, and he would go about among his friends whom he had known when he lived with old Barnet, helping and consoling them if they were sick or afflicted, and doing all the good a little boy could do, or by the help of his father making people happy when poverty or misfortune had made them miserable.

In the fine evenings they would sail out to sea in the old fishing boat; they did not fish, for they did not like to give pain to, and to destroy animals, but they would observe

* Whitsunday is the seventh Sunday after Easter, coming in late May or early June. Bartholomew Day was celebrated on 24 August, so both were suitable times for seaside holidays. Mary Shelley placed a small marginal question mark beside the line on which these dates occur.

the dancing waves, and the rocky shores; and if they stayed out long after sunset they saw how the stars came out one by one till the whole sky was covered with them.

During the other part of the year Dame Smithson lived in the old cottage. She was very sorry for what she had done, and loved Henry very much; and Henry never forgot that he had loved her once as a dear, good mother.

Many years after, Henry grew older and went abroad to foreign countries, and saw many beautiful scenes of rocks, and mountains, and trees, and rivers; yet he always loved in his heart his pretty cottage and thought it the most delightful place he had ever seen. It was very old as I have said before; and some time after when Dame Smithson died some of the moss-covered thatch fell off and let the water into the cottage during the rainy weather; it was too old to be repaired, and by degrees it fell all to pieces, and the sea washed it away as it fell, so that it quite disappeared.

When Henry returned from his travels he found his pretty cottage gone, his geraniums dead, and no wall left on which the sweet-smelling, yellow wallflowers could grow; this grieved him very much, yet he was pleased to find the red cliff, the waving trees, the freshwater rill, and the rock upon which he and his father used so often to sit, remained just the same as when he left them: though the boat had fallen to pieces in the cove, and the garden had run wild. He would not build another cottage there for it would have been too unlike old Barnet's that he had loved so well. But he built a house not far off where he placed to live a poor fisherman and his two children, who having lost his boat in a storm some months before and scarcely saved from drowning himself, was in great want and poverty. He built another boat for the little cove and often during his life came to visit the cliff, and the trees, and the rock; where he would sit and reflect on the life he had led while a little boy with old Barnet in the pretty, old, fisher's cot; and how his father came to visit and assist him when he was poor and helpless, not knowing him to be his son; and how on that very rock he had first discovered that he belonged to good, kind parents; with whom he now lived in content and happiness.

The End

Maurice

Showing the Author's Original Lineation, Pagination, Spelling, Corrections and Emendations

For Laurette from her friend Mrs Shelley

Maurice
or the
Fisher's Cot.
a tale.

Part I.

One sunday afternoon in the month
of September, a traveller entered the town
of Torquay, a seaport on the southern coast
of Devonshire. The afternoon was pleasant
and warm, and the waves of the sea, slightly
agitated by a breeze, sparkled under the
sun. The streets of the town were empty,
for the inhabitants after having been to
church were dining during the interval
between the services: so the traveller walked

on through the meaner streets of the town,
to the semicercle of houses that surrounds
the harbour; and then he paused at the door
of a neat-looking inn. The traveller wasn a
man about forty five years of age; he was |
remarkably erect in his person; alert and
even graceful in his walk; his hair was
black and curly, although a little fallen from
his temples; he was handsome, but somewhat
sun-burnt, & when he smiled he looked so
goodtempered and kind that you could not
see him without loving him. In dress and
manner he had the appearance of one
who had seen better days, w but who was
now poor; and he seemed serious, though
not depressed by poverty. His clothes were
coarse and covered with dust; he was on foot,
and had a wallet buckled on his back.

He entered the inn, and asking for din
ner, unbuckled his wallet, & sat down
to rest himself near the door. While he
was thus sitting a funeral passed bye:

it was evidently the funeral of a poor
person; the coffin was carried by some
peasants, and four mourners followed. ~~Thre~~
Three of these although serious, looked care
less and indifferent; the fourth was a boy |
of about thirteen years of age; he was
crying, & was so much taken up by his
own distress that he did not observe any
thing that passed near him. Somthing in
this boy's appearance attracted the traveller's
attention; and once when he ceased crying
and looked round towards the inndoor, the
traveller thought that he had seldom seen
so beautiful a youth. He turned to the land
lady, and asked,—"whose ~~wh~~ was that fu
neral? And who was the boy that accompa
nied it?"—

"That," replied the woman, "is the funeral
of old Barnet, the fisherman: and that boy
was a kind of servant or apprentice who
lived with him after the death of the old
dame, his wife."—

93

"Does he belong to this town?"—

"He does not, nor do I know from whence
he comes: he is the child of poor people or
his parents would never have sent him
to live in the cottage of old Barnet. The
neighbours say he is a good boy, but I know |
nothing about him.

The traveller sighed and said: "This
poor boy can be nothing to me, yet I
am much pleased with his appearance
and manner."—A young country man
who was dining at a table in a corner of
the room now rose, and said: "I live near
old Barnet's cottage, and know this boy
well; he is the best creature in the world,
and all who know him love him: as
you, sir, appear inquisitive about him,
I will, if you please, relate all I know
concerning him."—The traveller expressed
his assent and the country man began
thus:—

"Old Barnet's cottage is situated about

three miles from this town at the
foot of the cliff and overhung by a
few trees; it is very solitary and very
poor; the spring-tide comes up almost
to the steps of the door; & when the
wind blows the spray of the sea is dashed
against the windows. We neighbours often |
wondered how so old a cot could stand the stress of
weather; or being so near the sea that some
high ~~north~~ ^{south} winds do not blow the waves entirely
over it; but it is sheltered by the crag, and
being built on a ground somewhat higher
than the shore, out of the reach of the
most tempestuous waves, it stands there, as I
have known it stand ever since I was born,
an old weather beaten cot, the roof covered
with lichens and moss. Beside it is a little cove
where the fishing boat is kept, and there is an
out house where the nets and sails are ^{were}
placed when the old man returned from the
sea. A little fresh-water brook trickles from
the cliff, close to it, down into the sea, and

when I was a boy I used often to go and place
paper boats in this rill and watch them sailing
down to the sea where they were soon lost in
the great waves.

"Old Barnet and his dame lived here. He was
a most hardworking old man; early and late
you saw his little skiff at sea, and often
when no other boats s ventured out Barnet
would go and come back with fine, fresh fish for
the Torquay market. His dame was so lame that
she seldom moved ^{from} the old, worsted, highbacked
armchair where she used to sit mending the |
nets, and hearing a few children read, who
came to her from the neighbouring farm
houses. Our farm is only half a mile distant
from the cot and I am one of those who
learned to read in Dame Barnet's great bible.
She would not be paid for this, calling it merely
a good neighbourly turn; but every sunday I
used to bring her a basket of vegetables and
fruits, and every autumn she had a dozen
of our best cider.

"Well about ~~two~~ ^ayears ago this good woman
died, and all the children about wept at
her funeral: for besides hearing them read, which
she always did without scolding them (her only
punishment was not allowing us to visit her)
she would make nice worsted balls for them
and tell them stories of Goody Two Shoes & the
babes in the Wood, or sing to them the ballads
of Chevy Chase and many others which pleased
us who were older as ~~w~~ well as the children.
Besides she would do them a thousand services of
mending their clothes when torn by ~~accieden~~
accident and a thousand other little services
which made her a great favourite with all.
Barnet was very much grieved when she died:
she was of little help to him not being able to |
move from her arm chair without great diffi
culty; but when he came home ~~from~~ wet from
fishing, during the stormy winter days when every
wave almost broke over his boat, she would
contrive to have the fire lighted for him and the
little old cottage set in order for his ~~suff~~ supper.

But after her death when he returned from sea
he was obliged to go hungry and sometimes dripping wet
to the market at this town; and when he returned
he was not handy at cooking his food or cleaning
his room: besides he was now obliged to mend his
nets for himself, and that took up a great deal of
his time so that he did not catch so much fish
as before. All these things made him melancholy;
and he came about two months after his dame's
death to our farm with tears in his eyes, and
said he thought he should give up his fishing
and go up to this country to seek his fortune, for
that the old cottage under the cliff a had become
quite hateful to him since his dame's death.
He was a hale old man, but his hair was as
white as snow, and his back bent with age, so
that it was a piteous thing to hear him talk
of leaving his cot, and his boat, and t all that
he had in the world to seek his fortune among
strangers. My father comforted him, and made
him dine with us, & promised to send my sister |
Betsy sometimes to put his cottage in order:

so he went home with a lighter heart than
he came.

"The next day the wind blew into shore, and
the old man not being able to go out with his
boat, sat down on ~~the rock~~ a piece of rock
that formed a kind of seat near his cot, and
began to mend his nets. While he was thus em
ployed this same boy of whom we speak, whose
name is Maurice, came and sat down on the
rock near him. The boy was a stranger in this
part of the country, so after having saluted one
another they both remained silent for some time;
at length Maurice said:—"I think I could help
you in that work and as I have nothing I to
do I wish you would let me try."—

"Try, and welcome," said Barnet; "but how
is it that you have nothing to do? Good boys
ought to work; you do not belong to these
parts, and it is not well to see a boy of your
age wandering about the country alone."—"My
parents are poor," replied Maurice, "and not
being able to maintain me, I have tried to earn

my own livelihood; I have been brought up
to no trade, and have always been weakly &
unable to work hard. When I left home I |
came with a man I knew to a farm not far
distant, where they gave me work in plenty in
the fields, the stables and the barns. I worked hard
for my master was severe, so at length I fell
ill; then when I could work no longer they turned
me away, and I think I should have died had not
a poor woman taken care of me. She was so
poor that I would not be a burthen to her
any longer than was necessary, and now I am too
weak to work for my old master, so I am thrown
on the wide world, and would be much obliged to
any one who would help me either by giving
me such work as I ~~could~~ can do, or advising
me where I can go to get it; for I am willing,
and although I say it my self, I am honest and
have always been considered handy & ~~und~~ industrious."

"Old Barnet looked up in the boy's face;
you know how pretty a lad he is; he was then
sickly-looking and that made him a fitter object

for compassion: he has the sweetest voice in the
world and ~~th~~ all that he said seemed to go the
old man's heart. He thought;—I have no child ~~of~~
~~my own~~ upon earth: my only relation is a
brother who disdains a poor old fisherman
like me. My dame is dead, and I am alone
without anyone to help me if I am sick or to
say a cheerful, Good bye, God send you luck! when
I go a fishing. Surely this boy seems sent by heaven |
to me, and it seems to me that I love him
already as if he were my own son. He shall
stay with me; I can maintain him as I
maintained my poor wife who is gone: he
can put my cottage in order, mend my sails
& nets, and on windy evenings who knows
but he may be able to read the bible to me as
my dame used.

"This was a lucky thought; the bargain
was soon struck, and ever since Maurice
has lived with old Barnet in his cottage. He
is a good boy, honest, handy & clever: when
we came to know him all our house loved

him; he is able to read very tolerably, so
my little brothers went to him to learn
every sunday as they used to go to the Dame,
& no one can be more good tempered. He
made the old cottage quite another thing, clean
ing it, and mending the old chairs; white
washing the grate, and furbishing up the
pans & saucepans; & laying them in
or neat rows. He was always merry, always
at work, always ready to do a good turn for
the poor as well as the rich. Old Barnet
loved him better & better, and often thanked
God for the day when he first came to the |
cottage. Out at sea the old man saw through
the day the trees wave over his cottage roof,
and at night he could distinguish the candle
which Maurice placed at the window to
direct him where to steer. When he came to
shore the boy was always waiting there to help
him draw his boat up to the cove. Then in
winter he found a nice fire ready to dress his
supper, and the table spread with a coarse, old,

but clean cloth. In the morning when he went
to market, Maurice ~~clean~~ heaved the water
out of his boat, mended his nets, put his sails
in order, and said a smiling, "God give you
luck!" when he went to sea. They lived seve
ral months in this manner very happily,
and now a week ago old Barnet died."—

The countryman paused, and the travel
ler asked, "What will become of the boy?"—"I
do not know; but he ~~is~~ is so much loved that
I do not think he will come to want. For my
part I am now leaving the country for a few
weeks, for I am going to visit my grandmother
who lives at Sidmouth; but when I return the
first question I shall ask is what is become of
Maurice. I have told you a long story, Sir, but
I hope you will excuse me; you have now |
finished your dinner, and I will detain you
no longer. Good bye!"—"Thank you heartily.
Good day, and a pleasant journey to you,"—
was the reply, and the young man left the
inn.

The traveller remained sometime leaning
his head on his hand, thinking what he ~~shud~~
should do. He wanted very much to make
further enquiry about Maurice, but when
he thought of the business he had at Exeter
he could not resolve to delay his journey:
so after resting himself another hour, he
strapped on his wallet and left the inn,
following the Exeter road.

The next morning he arrived at this
city. By and bye I shall explain what
his business there was; but at present I
shall only say that having passed three
anxious days, he was obliged to give up his
business, and to determine to return whence
he came, that he might enquire whether
somthing had not happened in the mean
time that might help him; at the same
time he resolved on his way back, to visit
old Barnet's cottage, and to enquire what had |
become of Maurice, and to offer his ser
vices in placing him in some suitable

situation, where he might honestly get his
livelihood without being worked too hard.
And now leaving him to walk with his
wallet on his back along the road which
leads from Exeter to Torquay, let us take
a peep into the cottage under the cliff;
and see what has become of Maurice
and what help he is likely to get in his
misfortunes.

Part Second.

The three other mourners who had fol
lowed Old Barnet's funeral were the brother
of whom the country man had spoken, and
his two sons. After the funeral this brother,
who was a shopkeeper at Torquay and a money
loving man, spoke thus to Maurice:—"You,
it seems, were maintained by my poor brother,
and lived in his cottage: now you know by
the laws that since my brother died without
a will, all he was worth, the cottage and its
furniture, the boat and his nets are mine.
If they were not you are too young to follow
his trade, so there is no possible reason why you
should remain in the cottage. The neighbours
say you are an honest lad so I would not
be too hard upon you; you may stay in the
cottage one week, and you can employ ~~that~~
yourself
~~time~~ in seeking for a place: at the end of
∧

that time a friend of mine with his three
sons will come and live there, and having
bought the ~~ba~~ boat will carry on the fishing;
they will not want you for a servant, so
by that time you must remove. You are |
honest and therefore I need hardly
tell you that nothing in the cottage belongs to you, except what you brought
yourself, and that you will not be
allowed to take any thing away with you."—

Maurice thanked his old friend's brother
for allowing him to stay a week in the
cottage; he intended to have asked his
advise about what he ought to do, but
there was somthing so dry and forbidding
in his manner that he could not make
up his mind to speak, but went away,
walking sorrowfully along the shore
towards the old cottage. When he arrived he
thought that it looked so ~~det~~ desolate and
strange, that he had not the heart to enter
but sat down near the little fresh-water

brook, and watched the waves of the sea
breaking at his feet. For the first time for
several months he was idle; for it was no
use to mend the nets when his old protector
could not use them, or to get supper ~~b~~ ready
when he felt his heart too full to eat. He
cried for the loss of his dear Barnet till he
was quite tired, and then watched the sun
set in the blue sea; and half imagined that
perhaps Barnet was not dead, but out
fishing and that he could perceive his |
white sail far out at sea: but turning round
he saw the boat lying empty in the cove, &
then he knew it must be true that his only
friend was dead, and that he was ~~quite~~ now alone in
the world. At length quite exhausted by sorrow,
and feeling cold as the evening breeze arose and
whitened the sea with foam, he got up and
~~b~~ opening the cottage door, without eating any
supper or striking a light, he knelt down &
said his prayers and then went to bed.

Several days passed in this manner, and at

length he began to think that he ought not to
live this idle life any longer. The week ~~would soon~~ was almost gone
~~pass~~ when he must quit the cottage, and then
what should he do to earn bread to eat. Sometimes
he thought he would return to his parents, but
that he quickly determined not to do; and at
length he resolved to go to farmer Benson; the
father of the country man who related his story to
the traveller at Torquay. As he determined this
he sat on his accustomed stone near the fresh-
water rill, and looked at the ocean which was
unbroken by waves, and the sky where the sun
had set, and the evening star gleamed in the golden
light he had left behind him: the air was quite
calm and the murmuring of the tide, which was
going out, just broke the silence, while a few sea- |
gulls flew to their nests in the cliff over his head.
Maurice heard a step near him, and turning
round saw approach a kind, good-looking man
who was indeed the traveller whom I described
at the beginning of my story. The boy was
much surprised, for a stranger had never before

visited the cottage which was two miles from
any road: rising with his usual goodnature,
he asked him whether he had lost his way,
and offered to shew him the way to the nearest
town.

"I have not lost my way," said the traveller,
"I came to this cottage on purpose. I have
particular reasons for wishing to see it, and
would be much obliged to you if you could
afford me a bed to night."—"You are very welcome; the cottage is poor, but as the bed is
clean perhaps you will be content."—"I have
travelled too much, my good boy, not to be easily
satisfied. But do not rise; for the present let
us enjoy this pleasant evening here at the sea
side, watching the waves that leave so ~~smo~~
smooth a beach behind them. Your cottage is
built in a very pretty place."—"I think so
indeed, and although it is poor and very old yet
taking it altogether I do not think there is a
prettier in all the country round. The trees fall |
over & shelter it, a number of pretty flowers

grow beside the brook which comes running down
from the tall, red cliff. And nothing to my mind
can be more beautiful than the moss & lichens
yellow, green, white & blue that grow on the
old thatched roof, making it look finer than a
slated roof could possibly be. In the spring yellow
wall-flowers grow there, and the green before the
door is covered with daisies. Besides if you come
round to the other side where the cottage faces the
hill you will find a pretty lattice ~~with~~ grown
over with honeysuckles and several geraniums
in th a stand outside the window. The geraniums
were the great favourite of old Barnet's dame,
and he loved them for her sake. Mr Gregory
Barnet says that I must take nothing from
the cottage, and that I know very well; but if
farmer Benson will take me into his service
I will spend two shillings that I have in buying
the geraniums, if the man who is com~~m~~ing to
live here will be kind enough to sell them."—
"You intend then to leave this cottage?"—"I must.
I am not strong enough to manage the boat

and go out to sea, and so it is let to some fisherman,
next Sunday I go away; but I hope I shall get
work hereabouts; and I do not think I shall be |
unhappy, for I have seldom cried about my
own misfortunes when I have been ⩊ very
ill used indeed; and I do not dislike work
when it does not make me ill. I loved old
Barnet and liked my life here with him
and I cried very much when he died—but
if I can get work about a farm yard, I
hope in a month or two to sing as cheerfully
as I used when I saw his white sail among
the other boats which you ^see^ out at sea."

Maurice did not say all this at once,
but the stranger smiled so kindly, and asked
so many questions in so affectionate a manner,
that the boy was easily induced to open his
whole heart to him, and to talk about his
affairs as to an old friend. "I shall not
return to my parents," said he, "for I left deter
mining never more to see them till I could
earn my own bread. My father works hard and

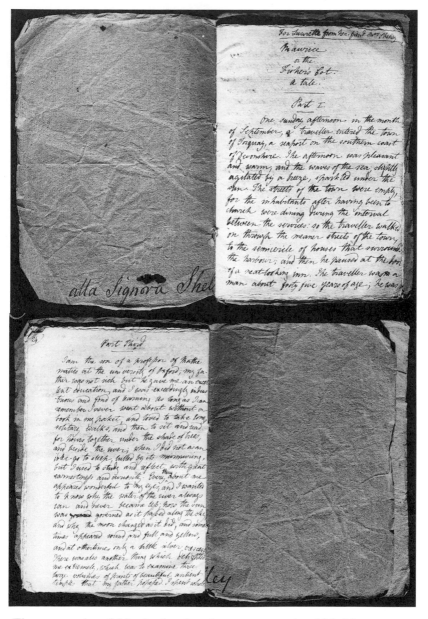

The manuscript of *Maurice* showing the paper cover in which Mary Shelley bound it in 1820, apparently taken from a parcel wrapping, since it bears the words 'alla Signora Shelley'; also the presentation inscription, 'For Laurette from her friend Mrs Shelley'.

(*above*) A contemporary print of Torquay, which Mary Shelley visited with Shelley in 1815, when she was pregnant with her son William, and made the setting for much of *Maurice*. (*upper right*) An idyllic view of Eton College, to which Henry/Maurice is sent after his rescue from poverty by his true parents. Although Shelley had been unhappy at Eton, he recalled boating parties on the river there with pleasure. (*lower right*) Mary made Ilfracombe on the north Devon coast the scene for the stealing of Henry/Maurice, and the home of his cruel foster-father.

Ilfracombe from the Torrs

unhappy, for I have seldom cried about my
own misfortunes when I have been very
ill used indeed; and I do not dislike work
when it does not make me ill. I loved old
Barnet and liked my life here with him
and I cried very much when he died – but
if I can get work about a farm yard, I
hope in a month or two to sing as cheerfully
as I used when I saw his white sail among
the other boats which you see out at sea.",

Maurice did not say all this at once
but the stranger smiled so kindly, and asked
so many questions in so affectionate a manner,
that the boy was easily induced to open his
whole heart to him, and to talk about his
affairs as to an old friend. "I shall not
return to my parents," said he, "for I left determining never more to see them till I could
earn my own bread. My father works hard and
wages are low, so being hardly able to get sufficient food for himself he was angry that he
had to maintain an idle boy, and my mother
is sufficiently vexed by him without my misfortunes being added to her cares. Unfortunately I
am a delicate boy and unable to work as he would
have me and have often been confined to
my bed with fevers. My father never would believe I was really ill & would beat me and

and send me to bed without my supper when I
could hardly stand. I do not mean to complain of
him, and though I have told all this to you who
are so kind, pray do not mention it to any one else.

I hus they chatted till the evening star had
set, and the sea became invisible through
darkness, except indeed the white heads of the
waves that broke near them; for the tide was
comming in and the rock on which they sat
began to be wetted by the spray: so they entered the
cottage, & supping on bread and salad, they presently after went to bed, the traveller telling the
boy that he would both break fast and dine
with him the following day.

Maurice awoke before light, and leaving his
guest sleeping soundly in bed he ran as fast as
he could to Torquay to buy some white bread
and potatoes and meat for their break fast and
dinner. He was obliged to spend for this provision
the two shillings with which he had intended to
purchase his dear geraniums, and this made him
a little sorrowful: but he was a cheerful,
happy-tempered boy, & consoled himself with thinking that he would work doubly hard to earn this
money before the next spring, and that he would
entreat the future tenant of the cottage to
take care of these pretty shrubs untill that time.

and when went abroad to foreign countries, &
saw many beautiful scenes of rocks, and
mountains, and trees, and rivers; yet he al
ways loved in his heart, his pretty cottage
and thought it the most delightful place he
had ever seen. It was very old as I have
said before; and some time after when
dame Smithson died some of the moss-covered
thatch fell off and let the water into the
cottage during the rainy wet weather; it was
too old to be repaired, and by degrees it fell
all to pieces, and the sea washed it away
as it fell, so that it quite disappeared.

When Henry returned from his travels
he found his pretty cottage gone, his gerani
ums dead, and no wall left on which
the sweet-smelling, yellow wall-flowers could
grow; this grieved him very much, yet he
was pleased to find the red cliff, the waving
trees, the fresh-water rill, and the rock upon
which he and his father used so often to
sit — remained just the same as before
when he left them: though the boat had
fallen to pieces in the cove, and the garden

(39) had run wild. He would not build another cottage there for it would have been
too unlike old Barnets that he had loved
so well. But he built a house not far
off, where he placed to live a poor fisherman
and his two children, who had lost his boat
in a storm some months before; ~~and had~~
~~& upon poor morning himself~~, was in great
want and poverty. He built another boat
for the little cove and often during his life
came to visit the cliff, and the trees, and
the rock; where he would sit and reflect
on the life he had led while a little boy
with old Barnet in the pretty, old, fisher's
cot; and how his father came to visit
and assist him when he was poor and
helpless, not knowing him to be his son;
and how on that very rock he had first
discovered that he belonged to good, kind
parents; with whom he now lived in
content and happiness.

The End

Richard Rothwell's portrait of the widowed Mary Shelley, painted some time before 1840, when she revisited Italy. She was there again in 1842, seeing Laurette and Nerina, and it was after this that she tried to help Laurette with her writing and translated part of one of her novels into English. Mary died in 1851.

wages are low, so being hardly able to get suffi

cient food for himself he ~~thinks~~ $\overset{\text{was}}{\wedge}$ angry that he

had to maintain an idle boy, and my mother

is suffitiently vexed by him without my misfor

tunes being added to her cares. Unfortunately I

am a delicate boy and unable to work as he would

have me and have often been confined to

my bed with fevers. My father never would be

lieve I was really ill & would beat me and |

and send me to bed without my supper when I

could hardly stand. I do not mean to complain of

him, and though I have told all this to you who

are so kind, pray do not mention it to any one else.

Thus they chatted till the evening star had

set, and the sea became invisible through

darkness, except indeed the white heads of the

waves that broke near them; for the tide was

com~~m~~ing in and the rock on which they sat

began to be wetted by the spray: so they entered the

cottage & supping on bread and salad, they pre-

sently after went to bed, the traveller telling the

boy that he would both break fast and dine

with him the following day.

Maurice awoke before light, and leaving his
guest sleeping soundly in bed he ran as fast as
he could to Torquay to buy some white bread,
and potatoes and meat for the breakfast and
                          ir
dinner. He was obliged to spend for this provision
the two shillings with which he had intended to
purchase his dear geraniums, and this made him
a little sorrowful: but he was a cheerful,
happy-tempered boy, & consoled himself with think
ing that he would work doubly hard to earn this
money before the next spring, and that he would
entreat the future tenant of the cottage to
take care of these pretty shrubs untill this time. |
                                    at
When he arrived at the cottage he found
the traveller seated on the rock on the beach;
they greeted one another kindly, and Maurice, at
the request of his guest, brought out a little
table on the sands, and placed their breakfast
on it in the open air; for it was a fine
warm morning without a cloud in the sky.
Their break fast was plain and countryfied

consisting of bread, a piece of cheese and a
basin of that nice clouted cream that they
make in Devonshire; and our two friends ate
so heartily of what was there that very
little remained. They then continued sitting on
the rock talking ~~together~~ of the pleasure of
living in the country, of seeing the pretty flowers
grow in the hedges and among the green grass; of
the beauty of the little birds, and the cruelty
of those who kill them: and the sweet life
it would be to take care of a nice farm,
not working too hard, but sufficient to become
healthy and strong through exercise; and in the
evening to read entertaining books, telling them of
how the earth is cultivated, and how various
countries bring forth various fruits: of the sea,
and how different voyages and discoveries have
been made on it: of the sky, and how the beau |
tiful stars which we see at night move, &
the signs they make of winter and summer.
The traveller told Maurice that there were
books more delightful than these which told

of what good and wise men had done a great
many years ago; how some had died to serve
their fellow creatures, and how ~~though~~ through
the exertions of these men every one had become
better, wiser and happier. Maurice said that
he had never read any book of that kind except
the bible, and that he had often cried over the
distress of Joseph, when he was sold to slavery,
and over the sorrow of David, when his son
Absolom revolted against him.

At length, after a pause, the traveller said
—"You talk my dear Maurice, of going to seek
for work at farmer Benson's: now what say
you if instead of this, you came and lived with
me. I would not task you too hard, but would
give you some of these pretty books to read, &
would do my best to make you happy."—Mau
rice looked up at the kind stranger and saw
him smiling benevolently upon him, "How good
you are!"—he replied.—"I will be good to you,"
said his guest, "but I am a stranger and |
you may be afraid to go away with ~~me~~ one

whom you ~~nene~~ never saw before. It is

late now for we have talked a long time, so

let us go in and ~~pl~~ prepare our dinner, and

afterwards ^we^ will come and sit here again and

I will tell you who I am; why I am travelling

on foot about the country; what my ^disappointments^ ~~hopes~~

have been, and what my hopes are."—

They did as he said. They made a good fire and

placed their meat and potatoes to boil. Maurice

filled a jug with clear water from the brook, and

the traveller took a small bottle of good wine

from his wallet. By noon the dinner was ready,

and after they had finished they sat down on

the rock, and the traveller ~~q~~ began his relation.

Part Third

I am the son of a professor of Mathe

matics at the university of Oxford; my fa-

ther was not rich but he gave me an excel

lent education, and I was exceedingly indus

-trious and fond of learning. As long as I can

remember I never went about without a

book in my pocket, and loved to take long,

solitary walks, and then to sit and read

for hours together under the shade of trees,

and beside the river; when I did not as an

idler go to sleep, lulled by its murmuring,

but I used to study and reflect with great

earnestness and curiosity. Every thing about me

appeared wonderful to my eyes, and I wanted

to know why the water of the river always

ran and never became less; how the sun

was ~~govered~~ governed as it passed along the sky,

and why the moon changed as it did, and some

times appeared round, and full, and yellow,
and at othertimes only a little silver crescent.
There was also another thing which delighted
me extremely, which was to examine three
large volumes of prints of beautiful antient
temples that my father possessed. I spent whole |
days in looking at these, and reading the accounts
of their dimensions and how they were built; for
I thought I should be the happiest creature in
the world if ever I should be able to build such
beautiful edifices as I saw represented in these
books. As I grew older I became fonder and
fonder of architecture, and as no knowledge is
gained without application I passed my whole
time in learning mathematics and those sciences
which best teach us how to erect edifices
such as the antients used to build. When I was
five and twenty my kind father sent me
abroad to ~~visit~~ Asia, Italy and Greece to visit
the remains of the old temples that still exist,
and I passed five years in this happy manner
dwelling among foreign nations, often in desart

places where the people do not live by sowing
& reaping corn and taking care of farms, as they
do here, but depend upon hunting for their
livelihood, leaving their native villages for months
together in search of game, and living a wild
life among the woods and mountains, while their
wives and daughters ~~sit~~ at ^remain ~~hop~~ home spinning
their own clothes, sitting in the open air, where
the winters are so mild that they have neither
frost or snow.

"When I returned to England I applied to |
business, and being a good architect I soon
became rich. When I thought I had money
enough I gave up my business and applied
my self to country labours and all kinds of
study, which I liked better than building churches
and bridges where the people have too little
taste or too little money to allow them to be
built in the beautiful manner I wished.

"I married at this time a lady, whom you
will soon see, my dear Maurice, and then you
will know how wise and good she is. Soon after

our marriage we had a little boy of whom we
were doatingly fond. All our joy was in watching
this little creature, who was as beautiful and good
as it was possible to be. When he was two years
old we made a journey during the summer
and f staid for a month at ~~Teignmouth~~ Ilfracombe
a sea port ~~about~~ more than fifty miles distance
from this place, and here a misfortune hap
pened to us since which we have never been
perfectly contented. It is now eleven years ago, but
I can never think of that time without being
unhappy.

"We used often to ride out my wife and I, and a
servant with our baby; and when we came to a
pretty place we used to leave the nurse and child
with the carriage while we took long walks in the |
country. One day we rode until we came to
the banks of a very pretty river; and telling the
nurse to wait for us, we walked on for several
miles, enjoying the pleasant weather, listening to the
singing of the birds in the elm trees which hung
over the river, and watching the little insects with

121

~~wh~~ wings of purple, green and gold that flew on
the surface of the water.

"When we returned we were dreadfully frighten
ed to find the nurse asleep among some hay and
no child near her. We awoke the woman and she
became pale with fear and trembled all over when
she found the child gone; since he had gone to sleep
in her arms, and she, without thinking of the
danger, and lulled to sleep by the sun, had at last
fallen asleep also. The first thing we did was to
run to the river;—but I will not describe, to
you, my little friend, the great grief we felt
during this search. We did not find our child, or
~~fin~~ see any remains of him near the water; on
the contrary we found one of his little shoes in a
field about a mile from the river, and this
made us think that perhaps he was stolen. We
spent many months in searching the whole country,
but in vain, we could not hear any tidings of
our dear, lost boy.

"For my part I have never given up hope |
that I shall one day find him again, for I

always felt convinced that he was not drowned.
So every year I spend two months in Devonshire
going over the whole county looking for him. I
dress myself meanly that I may enter the cottages
with greater freedom and make enquiries of
the country people in a familiar manner;
I walk about from village to village, and
never passe a solitary cottage without looking
at the children, and asking questions concern
-ing them.

"A fortnight ago I passed by a cottage
about five miles from Ilfracombe, at the
door of which stood a woman crying and
wringing her hands: I stopped and asked her what
was the matter, and she told me that her hus
band had died two days before, and that her only
son had been away ne a year and a half and
she did not know what had become of him. I
tried to console her, and told her that I also
was unhappy and had lost my only child while
a baby and had never found him again. I then
related to her my misfortune and was much

surprised to find her more distressed than
before, and when I described to her the great
grief of my wife, she cried out, "I am the cause of |
this! I am the wicked woman who stole your child!
I started at these words, and as soon as I could speak
I asked her what had become of my poor dear boy.
She then began to cry again, and said that it was
him she lamented when she told me that she
had not seen her only son for nearly two years.
She cried so much and appeared so distressed that
I was obliged to spend almost an hour before I
could console her, and then she told me how all
had happened.

"Her husband had been a sailor and they had
lived several years together and had had no children:
he was a bad man, and would beat and reproach
her for not having a child which made her very
unhappy, and she thought that she would be
perfectly happy w if heaven would bless her with
a son. At length once when her husband
went on a long voyage, she wrote to him a
month after his departure and told him that

she was with child. He staid away a long time,
and she continued to write and to tell falsehoods, how
the child was born and was thriving; and she did this
foolishly without thinking of the consequences, or
what her husband would say when he returned and
found no child. He was a sailor on board a king's
ship, and getting a wound in a battle which dis- |
abled him for a long time w he wrote to her
who was then living in London, to go down to
his native place at Ilfracombe, for that he
would leave his ship and go and live there the
rest of his days.

"She went down with a sorrowful heart not
knowing what she should say about her preten
ded child; and not liking to go among his relations,
who all expected to see a fine stout boy about
two years old, she took a mean lodging in a town
some miles off and went by a false name. She
passed two months in a very unhappy state of
mind, strolling about the country and not able
to determine as to what she would do, when one
day for our great misfortune she determined

to walk towards Ilfracombe to find out whether
her husband had arrived, and on her way she
found t our poor baby asleep in the arms of
his careless nurse.

"One wicked thing brings on another; and
she who had deceived her husband, and for two
years written a number of falsehoods, and
had become to have the habit of feeling guilty
and wrong, now made up her mind to steal this
child, not caring for the unhappiness of its parents.
She took him gently out of the nurse's ha arms,
and ran with him across the fields towards the |
town where she had been living for the last
two months. When she came near the town
she hid this my ownern the child under
some straw in a barn, and went as fast as
she could to her lodgings. She paid for them
and taking her mend bundle of clothes she went
back to the child and hid herself in the barn
all day. At night she began her journey. She
resolved to go to Plymouth and wait for
her husband whose ship was expected in that

port, and thus to quit the country near
Ilfracombe until her theft should be
forgotten. She walked all day and hid herself
at night for fear of being discovered. She
burned the child's good clothes and made it others
out of her own, preserving only a little coral
neck lace with his n̶ christian name engraved
on the clasp and the remaining shoe whose
fellow we found in the field and which we
have ever kept with great affection. She
lived six months at Plymouth before her
husband arrived and then they went together
and settled themselves in the cottage where
I found them. The woman soon loved our
poor boy as if it had been her own and |
took all possible care of it—caressing and tending
    him
on with the a̶f̶ tenderness of a mother.

"But people who a̶r̶e̶ do that which they ought
not to do seldom find that good come from
the crimes they commit which they expect. Our
poor boy had been accustomed to delicate fare
and gentle nursing; and whether it was that he

127

was now fed poorly and neglected (not through unkind
ness, but because she had not leisure to give him
the attention to which he had been accustomed with
us) whether it were on these accounts I know
not, but our little Henry became sickly and
delicate, and lost that fine bloom which first
tempted her to the wicked action of stealing him. Her hus
band who was a bad man and who had before
grumbled that he had no child, now became more
cross than ever, saying that the sickly brat would
never come to good, and that he was obliged to
maintain him by the sweat of his brow when
he would never be able to do the like for him
when he was old.

"The woman then said to me:—"I have
been very miserable as well as wicked: for
not only I felt great repentance at having |
taken this baby from his parents, but I found
my husband unkinder than ever, and that
instead of loving, he perfectly disliked the poor
child. Besides the dear fellow lost his health
and although the best creature in the

world and the ~~wos~~ most willing and clever,

yet he could do no hard work, and often had

fevers and other illnesses when my husband

grudged the doctor, and I used to sit crying by

his bedside thinking that if his rich parents had

still kept him he would not lie without help

on his sick bed.

"As he grew older my husband grew unkinder

and sometimes beat him because he could not

work, and treated him in so cruel a manner

that I dare not relate to you who are his father,

so one day Henry (for so I called him as by his broken

words I found his parents had named him) came

to me, and told me that farmer Jackson

had promised to get work for him, and that

he was determined to go and try if he could not

gain his own livelihood. I cried bitterly, but

could not alter his purpose, though then I

would have given all I had in the world to

find out who his rich parents were, that I |

might restore him. I gave him ^my^ blessing

and he went away and I have never heard

129

of him since!

"I will not tire you, my little friend,

with the account of my walks and anxieties

for this last fortnight; ~~Now~~ ^during^ ^which^ I have been

employed in going all over Devonshire tra

cing my lost child; my labours have been

unsuccessful. I am now going to return

to Dame Smithson to ask whether he has

returned to her. This is my story; do you consent

to come and live with me? If I never find

my darling boy you shall be a son to me,

and if I do find him——"

Maurice had listened to this relation

very attentively, and near the end his

eyes had streamed with tears and he shewed

every sign of interest and impatience: and

now when the traveller said these words he

threw himself into his arms and sobbed out—

"I am your son! Daddy Smithson is not

my father! I am your lost boy!"—And then

he told him how he had always considered |

Dame Smithson his mother, and how kind

to him and fond of him she was; and
how her husband had made him perfectly
miserable so that he had determined never
to go home again until he should be able
to earn his bread for himself. He said that
he had called himself Maurice because
he was afraid that the cruel man whom
he ~~called~~ ^{thought} his father might come to that
part of the country and find him out and
beat and illuse him as he used to do at
home.

Now nothing could be happier than the
traveller and his dear son as they sat
together by the sea-side, talking about
what they would do and the joy of his poor
mother when she should see him again.
Henry cried for joy when he thought of
the happy life they should lead, reading
delightful books, living with a kind
father and mother, and having no care
upon earth but that of obeying them
and making them happy. They went that

very evening to Torquay, and hiring a chaise
they rode towards the traveller's home; and |
never rested until they arrived and Henry
was in his mother's arms.

And what became of the old mossed-roofed
cottage by the sea-side? Why, at Henry's request
his father bought it, and the ba boat, and
the geraniums, and all that belonged to it from
Mʳ Gregory Barnet. They could not live there
because Henry was obliged to go to Eton to
school; and his father's house was near Windsor
park, close to the school, so that he always
lived with his dear parents. But in the
Whitsuntide and Bartholomewtide holidays they
wend went down to Devonshire to visit
the pretty cottage and lived in it two months
every p year. It was too small for any ser
vants to come with them, so Henry put on
a coarse country dress, and his father clothed
himself as he used when he travelled about the
country to seek for his child. Thh They took care of
the garden, bought their own food, coock cooked

their own dinner; and when the weather was
fine and the ~~sun~~ sun shone they sat on
the rock near the fresh-water rill and talked
about all the ~~de~~ beautiful things they had seen |
or would one day see, or read delightful
books whose knowledge and lessons made them
both wiser ~~hand~~ and happier. When they
were at this cottage Henry always went by
the name of Maurice, and he would go
about among his ~~old~~ friends whom he had
known when he lived with $\overset{\text{old}}{\underset{\wedge}{\text{Barnet}}}$ helping
and consoling them if they were sick or
afflicted, and doing all the good a little boy
could do, or by the help of his father making
people happy when poverty or misfortune
had made them miserable.

In the fine evenings they would sail out to
sea in the old fishing boat; they did not fish
for they did not like to give pain to, and to
destroy animals, but they would observe the
dancing waves, and the rocky shores; and if they
staid out long after sunset they saw how the

stars came out one by one till the whole
sky was covered with them.

During the other part of the year Dame
Smithson lived in the old cottage. She was
very sorry for what she had done, and loved
Henry very much; and Henry never forgot
that he had loved her once as a dear, good
mother.

Many years after, Henry grew older |
and ~~when~~ went abroad to foreign countries, &
saw many beautiful scenes of rocks, and
mountains, and trees, and rivers; yet he al
ways loved in his heart his pretty cottage
and thought it the most _{delightful} ~~beautiful~~ place he
had ever seen. It was very old as I have
said before; and some time after when
Dame Smithson died some of the moss-covered
thatch fell off and let the water into the
cottage during the rainy ~~we~~ weather; it was
too old to be repaired, and by ~~de~~ degrees it fell
all to pieces, and the sea washed it away
as it fell, so that it quite disappeared.

When Henry returned from his travels
he found his pretty cottage gone, his gerani
-ums dead, and no wall left on which
the sweet-smelling, yellow wall-flowers could
grow; this grieved him very much, yet he
was pleased to find the red cliff, the waving
trees, the fresh-water rill, and the rock upon
which he and his father used so often to
sit—remained just the same as ~~before~~
when he left them: though the boat had
fallen to pieces in the cove, and the garden |
had run wild. He would not build ~~an~~ ano
-ther cottage there for it would have been
too unlike old Barnet's that he had loved
so well. But he built a house not far
off where he placed to live a poor fisherman
and his two children, who ha~~d~~ lost his boat
in a storm some months before, ~~and scarcely~~
~~h saved from drowning himself~~, was in great
want and poverty. He built another boat
for the little cove and often during his life
came to visit the cliff, and the trees, and

the rock; where he would sit and reflect
on the life he had led while a little boy
with old Barnet in the pretty, old, fisher's
Cot; and how his father came to visit
and assist him when he was poor and
helpless, not knowing him to be his son;
and how on that very rock he had first
discovered that he belonged to good, kind
parents; with whom he now lived in
content and happiness.

———————————

The End

———————————

APPENDIX

'Twelve Cogent Reasons for Supposing P. B. Sh–ll–y
to be the D–v–l Inc–rn–t–'
by Lady Mountcashell*

> 'Tis often thought by learned men
> That Satan walks the earth again;
> And some ev'n go so far's to say
> He ne'er one hour has been away
> Since first to Eden's garden went he
> As Dame Eve's Cavalier Servente;
> But always in one form or other
> Contrives the Lord's elect to bother.
> I oft with holy zeal had tried
> To find him out; but he defied
> My efforts almost half a century,
> And (though I scarcely dared to venture) I
> Still sometimes thought a doubtful matter
> This Devil, who makes such a clatter
> Among the Saints & the Saintesses,
> And teaches them such pranks (God bless us!)
> As frighten unbelieving sinners,
> And give the holy priests good dinners.
> I must confess, for want of persons
> (Who in this popish land are scarce ones)
> Churches with pews (for *pews* here none add)

* This text is taken from a typed transcript in the Cini archive.

Un-Crucifixed & un-Madonna'd,
Free from the sad abomination
Of odorif'rous exhalation;
Breathing alone such vapours pure,
As pious Protestants endure,
To shew their faith in holy writ;
In Luther's or in Calvin's wit.
For want of all these saving aids
I thought (how conscience me upbraids!)
That Satan was a mere non-entity,
A shadow which had no identity,
The blind caprice of troubled rain
Seeking for something wise in vain.
Such were my silly dreams when first
Conviction met me, and disperst
All doubts; shewing that but too well I
Might see the Devil in P. B. Shelley.
Of this sad truth are proofs abundant,
To write one half would be redundant;
But twelve I will select, to shew
That Satan still walks to & fro,
And without doubt's the cause of all
The ills which Kings & *Queens* befall.

Proof 1st   First, all who see his face, observe
A sensibility of nerve
That's quite unnatural to man,
And shews the Devil soon began
To make his nest in Shelley's gizzard,
Who straight became a dreadful wizard.

Proof 2nd   Seeking good Christians to devour,
He clapped his claw in early hour
On orthodoxy's lulling preacher;

Made him a philosophic teacher,
To lead his pious flock astray
In toleration's wicked way.

Proof 3rd Then set gold traps for honour'd sage,
And filled his mind with Mammon's rage,
So that the voice which gained applause
While erst employed in virtue's cause,
And oft so well of *Justice* spoke,
Can now no power but Wealth invoke.

Proof 4th Next good dull folks (in *Study* small)
Frugal in food, *in hats*, in all,
He lends *three hundred* foul temptations;
So wafts them off to distant nations,
To *cut a dash in Paris* town,
Which surely marks them for his own—

Proof 5th Who hears him talk of Hell's delights,
(That red hot furnace which affrights
Those worthy souls whose faith ne'er fails
In fire & brimstone, horns & tails)
And sees him chuckle at the thought
Of myriads, who must there be brought,
Can never question that his home
Is somewhere near that dev'lish dome.

Proof 6th All unknown tongues he speaks at will;
And this another proof is still,
For Satan ever has been known
To strange outlandish lingos prone:
And when exorcised by a Priest,
Has always talked Latin at least.

Proof 7th Oft he cajoleth simple souls
When with kind soothing looks, he strolls
About, and helps the sick & poor;

139

Feeds one & pays for t'others cure.
Little they know the reason why;
He fears lest these *in grace* should die,
And so to Heaven from him escape,
Though Hell with all its might should gape.

Proof 8th Whene'er he meets with folks so wicked
That such black crimes they do not stick at
As living without visit-paying,
Or daily gossipping, or praying;
Who laugh at holy priests & kings
And queens & other sacred things;
With these he feels in near relation,
Brothers & sisters of damnation—

Proof 9th But when he meets the Lord's elect
None who behold but must suspect
That poetry puts him to pain
For, as if he were a snake again
He twists & winds about, & tries
To shun the gaze of Christian eyes;
And when no other means avail
Springs from his chair & turns his tail.

Proof 10th With learning of a Grecian sage,
And genius of an Attic age,
No mark of arrogance he shews,
As would the mortal wight disclose.
So 'tis not possible that he
Can other than old Satan be—

Proof 11th In holy places ev'n he lurks
To carry on his sinful works.
With looks as harmless as a child,
And words of blasphemy so mild,
Corrupts the spouses of the Lord

And makes them speak in tongues abhorred—
All mischief quietly he plans,
The flame of every ill he fans;
Makes nubile spinsters lose their beauty:
Proof 12th And matrons old forget their duty.
Witness alas! this dogg'rel rhyme;
Whose writer should have at this time
Been otherwise employed: and now
Can only wish it had been so—
But when the Devil drives, they say
No mortal can direct the way—

NOTES

1. *Mary Shelley: Collected Tales and Stories*, edited by Charles E. Robinson, was published by the Johns Hopkins University Press in 1976.
2. According to J. M. S. Tompkins's study of the late eighteenth-century novel, Henry was by far the most popular name for writers of fiction of the period: 'eighty per cent of the heroes are called Henry'. It seems extraordinary, but see her *The Popular Novel in England 1770–1800* (1932; repr. 1969), pp. 57–8n. She adds, 'William, on the other hand, is a name of dubious, often villainous, complexion.' Mary's choice of names for her characters is sometimes surprising, as when, for instance, she uses her own infant son William's name for the little William who is murdered in *Frankenstein*.
3. Mary forgave Eton's treatment of her husband enough to make it her first choice for their son Percy Florence later, although she was dissuaded by Shelley's father on the grounds that the boy might be teased there – like his father. She sent him to Harrow.
4. We know nothing about this 1815 visit beyond that it was made. Mary used the Cornish coast in her last novel, *Falkner*, in which an orphaned child lives beside the sea with a poor foster-mother before being rescued by a father-figure. The Cornish coast was also used in her story of 1833, *The Smuggler and His Family*, in which a father tries to make his son follow him into smuggling. It was written especially for a fund-raising publication, and is remote from *Maurice* in subject and tone.
5. *Matilda* remained unpublished until 1959.

143

6. The 'Note on Peter Bell the Third', written by Mary Shelley in 1839 for the second edition of her husband's poems, mentions that 'a critique on Wordsworth's *Peter Bell* reached us at Leghorn' in 1820, and that 'no man ever admired Wordsworth's poetry more; – he read it perpetually, and taught others to appreciate its beauties'.

7. Document written by Lady Mountcashell in Pisa in April 1818. It is reproduced in Edward C. McAleer, *The Sensitive Plant* (1958), p. 8.

8. The evidence for the existence of Elena Adelaide Shelley was found by Professor Alberto Tortaglione, searching in Naples on behalf of the Shelley biographer Newman Ivey White, in 1936. There is a birth registration, signed by Shelley and naming himself as father and Mary as mother, and giving her birth as 27 December 1818; a baptismal certificate for 27 February 1819, again naming Shelley and Mary as her parents, and naming the midwife also; and a certificate of death, saying that 'Elena Schelly of Naples' died on 9 June 1820, aged fifteen months and twelve days, at her home. The informants were a cheesemonger and a potteryman, and the child is described as the daughter of 'Bercy Schelly' and 'Maria Gebuin', both domiciled at Leghorn.

9. Lady Mountcashell's words about Mary Wollstonecraft – whom she does not name, although she is clearly referring to her – are also taken from the document quoted above, written in 1818. They appear on p. 5 of McAleer's *The Sensitive Plant*.

10. Lady Mountcashell to William Godwin, 8 Sept. [n.y. but 1801], unpub. MS, Abinger deposit, c. 507/5, Bodleian Library.

11. Charles Kegan Paul, *William Godwin, His Friends and Contemporaries* (1876), pp. 369–70.

12. Information from Catherine Wilmot's journal, printed in *An Irish Peer on the Continent 1801–3*, Thomas U. Sadleir, ed. (1920).

13. Unpub. MS poems in Cini archive.

14. Lady Mountcashell to Denys Scully, 27 July 1806, Munich, letter 149, Brian MacDermot, *The Catholic Question in Ireland and England 1798–1882: The Papers of Denys Scully* (1988), p. 133.
15. ibid.
16. ibid., pp. 133–4.
17. Unpub. MS, Cini archive.
18. Unpub. MS, Cini archive.
19. Lady Moira to Denys Scully, 17 Sept. 1807, letter 158, MacDermot, *The Catholic Question in Ireland and England 1798–1882*, pp. 145–6.
20. Cini archive, only partly published in McAleer, *The Sensitive Plant*, p. 199.
21. Lady Mountcashell's document of Apr. 1818; these words, McAleer, *The Sensitive Plant*, p. 7.
22. McAleer, *The Sensitive Plant*, pp. 7–8.
23. Claire Clairmont to Lord Byron, 27 for 26 Apr. 1818, *The Clairmont Correspondence*, Marion Kingston Stocking, ed. (1995), vol. I, p. 115.
24. 8 Jan. 1819, MS letter in French in Abinger deposit, c. 811/3, Bodleian Library, only partly published: 'je ne pouvais accoutumer la petite a ne pas se salir la nuit . . . Allegra est devenue tranquille et sérieuse comme une petite vieille, ce qui nous peine beaucoup.'
25. Marion Kingston Stocking suggests a new possibility in an appendix to her *The Clairmont Correspondence*. The suggestion is that Shelley had a passing sexual fling, just before leaving London in the spring of 1818, with a young English lady who pursued him with her admiration, became pregnant as a result, and followed him to Italy. Adelaide Constance Campbell *may* have been travelling in Italy with her mother Lady Charlotte Campbell, although there is no certainty that she was. What is known for certain is that in March 1818 Lady Charlotte

married her chaplain, the Reverend Edward John Bury, who, as it happens, graduated from Oxford in 1811, the year Shelley was expelled from the university for atheism. The possibility of a link is there, and the name is good, but nothing is proved. The sources for the story of Shelley's 'scrape' are Claire Clairmont's remarks in old age to Edward Silsbee, and Shelley's cousin Thomas Medwin.

The affair remains wrapped in mystery. Not surprisingly, Shelley did his best to conceal whatever happened. Accused by blackmailing servants of fathering Elena on Claire, he denied it vehemently. Mary also firmly denied this version, when he asked her to do so; but neither offered any explanation as to the child's real parentage, and Shelley cuts a curious figure when he protests that he would never commit the 'unutterable crime' of 'abandoning a child'. It is, after all, exactly what he did in this case.

26. 4 Aug. 1819, *The Journals of Mary Shelley*, Paula R. Feldman and Diana Scott-Kilvert, eds. (1987), vol. I, p. 293.

27. Claire Clairmont, cited in McAleer, *The Sensitive Plant*, pp. 3–4, giving as his source Edward Dowden, *The Life of Percy Bysshe Shelley* (1887), vol. II, p. 317.

28. 14 Nov. [1819], unpub. MS, Abinger deposit, c. 517/2, Bodleian Library.

29. Both from Lady Mountcashell to Percy Bysshe Shelley, 14 Nov. 1819, unpub. MS, Abinger deposit, c. 517/1, Bodleian Library.

30. Lady Mountcashell to Mary Shelley, Friday 14 [Jan. 1820], letter 7, unpub. MS, Abinger deposit, c. 517/2, Bodleian Library.

31. Thursday, 27 Jan. 1820, *The Journals of Claire Clairmont*, Marion Kingston Stocking, ed. (1968), p. 119.

32. Claire Clairmont to Lord Byron, 23 Apr. 1820, *The Clairmont Correspondence*, vol. I, p. 143.

33. Claire Clairmont to Lord Byron, 1 May 1820, *The Clairmont Correspondence*, vol. I, p. 145.
34. This was published in 1820. Claire Clairmont was reading it in Pisa on 18 July, two days before she rode with Laurette to visit Mary at Livorno.
35. Nora Crook points out that Mary Shelley made no entries in her journal between 6 and 9 August, and that her habit of summarizing the activities of blank days on the day she resumes her journal could indicate that she had been writing and copying out *Maurice* over a five-day period. I am sure this is right, and that 'Wrote a story for Laurette' on 10 August covers the previous days' work on it. The story is too carefully composed to be the work of a single day.
36. Percy Bysshe Shelley to Mary Shelley, 15 Aug. 1821, cited by McAleer, *The Sensitive Plant*, p. 161.
37. Mary Shelley to Claire Clairmont, Mar. 1822, *The Letters of Mary Wollstonecraft Shelley*, Betty T. Bennett, ed. (1980–88), vol. I, p. 226.
38. ibid, pp. 225–6.
39. Claire Clairmont to Lord Byron, 18 Feb. 1822, *The Clairmont Correspondence*, vol. I, p. 170.
40. Claire Clairmont to Mary Shelley, 9 Apr. 1822, *The Clairmont Correspondence*, vol. I, p. 171.
41. I am struck by the fact that different authorities give *three* different dates for the death of Allegra in April 1822. Rosalind Glynn Grylls (*Mary Shelley*, 1938) gives 19 April, as does Newman Ivey White (*Shelley*, New York 1940, London 1947), repeated by Robert Gittings (*Claire Clairmont and the Shelleys*, 1992), Betty T. Bennett (*The Letters of Mary Wollstonecraft Shelley*, vol. I), Marion Kingston Stocking (*The Journals of Claire Clairmont* and *The Clairmont Correspondence*) and Mario Curelli (*Una Certa Signora Mason*, 1997). Iris Origo (*A Measure of Love*, 1957) gives 21 April, repeated

by Phyllis Grosskurth (*Byron: The Flawed Angel*, 1997); Grosskurth follows Doris Langley Moore (*Lord Byron: Accounts Rendered*, 1994) in saying he received the news of his daughter's death on the 22nd. Byron himself asked to have '20th April' inscribed on Allegra's gravestone. Peter Quennell (*Byron: A Self-Portrait*, 1950), Leslie Marchand (*Byron: A Biography*, 1957), Michael Foot (*The Politics of Paradise*, 1988) and the catalogue to the Victoria & Albert *Byron* exhibition of 1974 repeat 20 April. In vol. VII of the Carl H. Pforzheimer Library's *Shelley and His Circle* (8 vols., 1961–86), Doucet Devin Fischer gives 20 April also, with a time, 10 p.m., but no source. 20 April certainly seems the most likely date. Fischer refers to a manuscript letter from Teresa Guiccioli to Byron, which tells him she has given the news to Mary Shelley on the 23rd, for Mary to pass on to Shelley; and, indeed, Mary Shelley's *Journal* has 'Evil news' on the 23rd.

The discrepancies in the dating of an event at the centre of the lives of Byron and the Shelley circle, so often worked over by scholars, are curious. As Langley Moore wrote, 'Infant life was cheap': and perhaps the dating of infant death still seems relatively unimportant. There has also been a reluctance to cast blame on Byron for his neglect and his refusal to heed Claire's warnings; or to give her credit for the efforts she made to save Allegra.

42. Lady Mountcashell to Lord Byron, early 1823, cited in McAleer, *The Sensitive Plant*, p. 174.

43. Lady Mountcashell to Mary Shelley, 13 Jan. 1823, unpub. MS, Abinger deposit, c. 517/2, Bodleian Library.

44. Lady Mountcashell to Mary Shelley, 25 Feb. 1823, unpub. MS, Abinger deposit, c. 517/2, Bodleian Library.

45. Lady Mountcashell to Mary Shelley, spring 1824, cited in McAleer, *The Sensitive Plant*, p. 191.

46. Lady Mountcashell to Mary Shelley, cited in McAleer, *The Sensitive Plant*, p. 202.

47. Cited in McAleer, p. 200, from the Cini MSS.

48. Claire Clairmont to Mary Shelley, 26 Oct. 1832, *The Clairmont Correspondence*, vol. I, p. 290.

49. I am grateful to the Director of the Archives of the French Diplomatic Service at the Quai d'Orsay for sending me the file on Galloni.

50. Archives of the Quai d'Orsay; Mary Shelley to Maria Gisborne, 17 July 1834, *The Letters of Mary Wollstonecraft Shelley*, vol. II, p. 210.

51. William Tighe to Laurette Tighe, 1831, unpub. MS, Cini archive.

52. Claire Clairmont to Mary Shelley, 26 Oct. 1832, *The Clairmont Correspondence*, vol. I, p. 291.

53. ibid.

54. Claire Clairmont to Mary Shelley, 13 July 1845, *The Clairmont Correspondence*, vol. II, p. 452.

55. Claire Clairmont to Jane Hogg, 1 Feb. 1833, *The Clairmont Correspondence*, vol. I, p. 296.

56. Claire Clairmont to Mary Shelley, 15 Sept. 1833, *The Clairmont Correspondence*, vol. I, p. 301.

57. Mary Shelley to Maria Gisborne, 17 July 1834, *The Letters of Mary Wollstonecraft Shelley*, vol. II, p. 210.

58. Claire Clairmont to Mary Shelley, 2 June 1835, *The Clairmont Correspondence*, vol. II, p. 320.

59. Laurette Galloni to William Tighe, 17 Dec. 1835, unpub. MS, Cini archive.

60. Laurette Galloni to William Tighe, 9 Oct. 1835, unpub. MS, Cini archive.

62. ibid.

62. Laurette Galloni to William Tighe, 29 Jan. 1836, unpub. MS, Cini archive.

63. ibid.

64. Laurette Galloni to William Tighe, 16 Feb. 1837, unpub. MS, Cini archive.

65. Mary Shelley to John Cochrane, 22 Dec. 1829, *The Letters of Mary Wollstonecraft Shelley*, vol. II, p. 97. Stendhal made his own version of the story of the Cenci, which he took from sixteenth- and seventeenth-century manuscripts he found when he was at Civitavecchia in 1834. *Les Cenci* was published only after his death (and Mary Shelley's), in 1855, together with other Italian stories from the manuscripts, *Vittoria Accoramboni, L'Abbesse de Castro*, etc., under the title of *Chroniques italiennes*.

66. Laurette Galloni to William Tighe, 2 Sept. 1836, unpub. MS, Cini archive.

67. Laurette Galloni to William Tighe, 9 Dec. 1836, unpub. MS, Cini archive.

68. Mary Shelley to Marianna Hammond, 23 Jan. 1843, *The Letters of Mary Wollstonecraft Shelley*, vol. III, p. 56; Mary Shelley to Claire Clairmont, *The Letters of Mary Wollstonecraft Shelley*, vol. III, p. 62.

69. Mary Shelley to Claire Clairmont, 15 Apr. 1843, *The Letters of Mary Wollstonecraft Shelley*, vol. III, p. 69.

70. Claire Clairmont to Mary Shelley, 2 June 1843, *The Clairmont Correspondence*, vol. II, p. 377.

71. Mary Shelley to Marianna Hammond, Mar. 1846, *The Letters of Mary Wollstonecraft Shelley*, vol. III, p. 281.

72. English translation of Claire Clairmont to Bartolomeo Cini, 22 Feb. 1835, *The Clairmont Correspondence*, vol. II, pp. 317–18.

BIBLIOGRAPHICAL NOTE

My point of departure was Mary Shelley. I consulted unpublished letters to her, as well as her papers in the Abinger deposit in the Bodleian Library in Oxford. Of published works, I used her biographical notes to P. B. Shelley's *Poetical Works* (Oxford edition, 1970). Betty T. Bennett's three volumes of *The Letters of Mary Wollstonecraft Shelley* (1980–88) were indispensable sources of information, as were the two volumes of *The Journals of Mary Shelley*, edited by Paula R. Feldman and Diana Scott-Kilvert (1987). I also relied on the eight volumes of *The Selected Works of Mary Shelley*, edited by Nora Crook (1996); *The Collected Tales and Stories of Mary Shelley*, edited by Charles E. Robinson (1976), and the Carl H. Pforzheimer Library's eight-volume *Shelley and His Circle* (1961–86). Marilyn Butler's introduction to the Penguin edition of *Frankenstein* (1994) is a useful one.

Edward Dowden's two-volume *Life of Percy Bysshe Shelley* (1886), Newman Ivey White's *Shelley* (2 vols., New York, 1940; London 1947) and Richard Holmes's *Shelley: The Pursuit* (1974) were all helpful. Charles Kegan Paul's *William Godwin, His Friends and Contemporaries* (1876) remains a good source of information and letters relating to Mary Shelley's childhood. There is also Rosalind Glynn Grylls's *Mary Shelley* (1938) and Muriel Spark's *Child of Light: A Reassessment of Mary Shelley*, a pioneering book when it appeared in 1951; a revised edition came out in 1987.

On Lady Mountcashell, the Cini archive is a rich source of unpublished letters, poems and papers. There is only one biography of her, Edward C. McAleer's *The Sensitive Plant* (1958). Kegan Paul's *Godwin* has some material on her. *An Irish Peer on the Continent 1801 –*

3 (the journal of Catherine Wilmot), edited by Thomas U. Sadleir (1920), is informative about the early part of the Mountcashells' continental tour. Some of her letters appear in Brian MacDermot's *The Catholic Question in Ireland and England 1798–1822: The Papers of Denys Scully* (1988). Mario Curelli's *Una Certa Signora Mason* (1997) has a good account of some of her unpublished fiction. Her *The Sisters of Nansfield* (1824) is, at the time of writing, catalogued under 'Anon? Charles Lamb' in the British Library.

On Claire Clairmont I used Marion Kingston Stocking's fine edition of *The Journals of Claire Clairmont* (1968) – one of the books that awoke my interest in the history of the group – and her two-volume *The Clairmont Correspondence* (1995). I also referred to Rosalind Glynn Grylls's biography *Claire Clairmont* (1939) and Robert Gittings's and Jo Manton's *Claire Clairmont and the Shelleys* (1992), although sadly this is not entirely reliable.

On Allegra I consulted Iris Origo's essay in *A Measure of Love* (1957), Leslie Marchand's *Byron's Letters and Journals* (12 vols., 1973–82), and many biographies of Byron.

For Laurette Tighe's history I have drawn extensively on the Cini archive again, guided by Cristina Dazzi's expert knowledge of it. For Laurette's husband Galloni's career and life, I consulted the Archives of the French Diplomatic Service at the Quai d'Orsay. Of her works, I have been able to read *La Spettatrice* by 'Sara' (4 vols., Milan, 1868), containing essays and a novella, *L'Ideale et la Scelta*; *Una Madre* (1857); *Le Due Fidanzate* (1864); and *Debole e Tristo* (1875).

FAMILY TREES

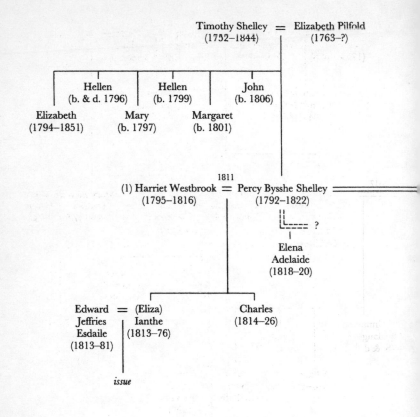

The Family Tree of Mary Shelley

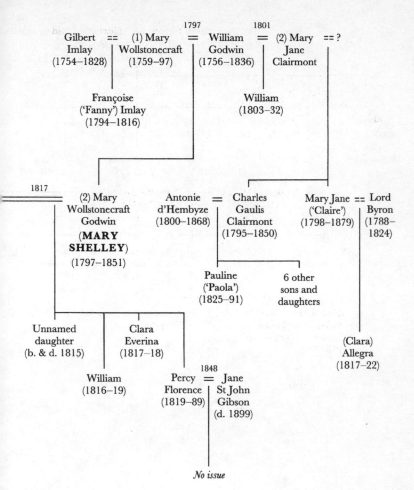

Gilbert Imlay (1754–1828) == (1) Mary Wollstonecraft (1759–97) = William Godwin (1756–1836) [1797] = (2) Mary Jane Clairmont [1801] == ?

Françoise ('Fanny') Imlay (1794–1816)

William (1803–32)

[1817] == (2) Mary Wollstonecraft Godwin (**MARY SHELLEY**) (1797–1851)

Antonie d'Hembyze (1800–1868) = Charles Gaulis Clairmont (1795–1850)

Mary Jane ('Claire') (1798–1879) == Lord Byron (1788–1824)

Pauline ('Paola') (1825–91)

6 other sons and daughters

Unnamed daughter (b. & d. 1815)

Clara Everina (1817–18)

William (1816–19)

Percy Florence (1819–89) = [1848] Jane St John Gibson (d. 1899)

(Clara) Allegra (1817–22)

No issue

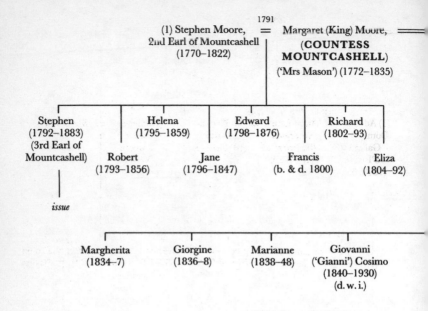

1791
(1) Stephen Moore, = Margaret (King) Moore, ===
2nd Earl of Mountcashell (**COUNTESS
(1770–1822) MOUNTCASHELL**)
('Mrs Mason') (1772–1835)

| Stephen (1792–1883) (3rd Earl of Mountcashell) | Helena (1795–1859) | Edward (1798–1876) | Richard (1802–93) |

Robert (1793–1856)   Jane (1796–1847)   Francis (b. & d. 1800)   Eliza (1804–92)

issue

Margherita (1834–7)   Giorgine (1836–8)   Marianne (1838–48)   Giovanni ('Gianni') Cosimo (1840–1930) (d. w. i.)

The Family Tree of Lady Mountcashell

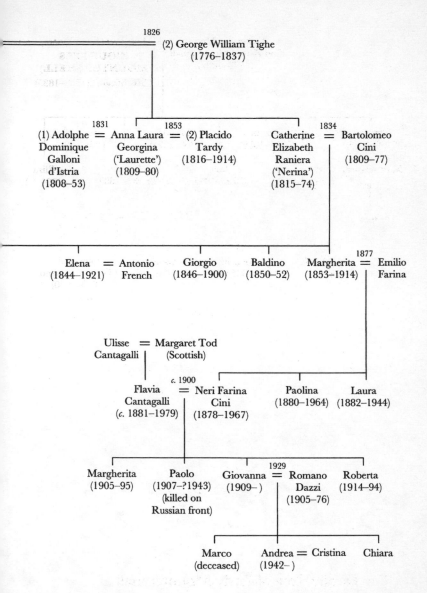

1826
(2) George William Tighe
(1776–1837)

(1) Adolphe = Anna Laura = (2) Placido   Catherine = Bartolomeo
Dominique   Georgina   Tardy   Elizabeth   Cini
Galloni   ('Laurette') (1816–1914) Raniera   (1809–77)
d'Istria   (1809–80)   ('Nerina')
(1808–53)   (1815–74)
      1831   1853   1834

Elena = Antonio   Giorgio   Baldino   Margherita = Emilio
(1844–1921) French   (1846–1900) (1850–52) (1853–1914) Farina
                                              1877

Ulisse = Margaret Tod
Cantagalli   (Scottish)

Flavia = Neri Farina   Paolina   Laura
Cantagalli   Cini   (1880–1964) (1882–1944)
(c. 1881–1979) (1878–1967)
        c. 1900

Margherita   Paolo   Giovanna = Romano   Roberta
(1905–95)   (1907–?1943) (1909–)   Dazzi   (1914–94)
             (killed on   (1905–76)
             Russian front)   1929

Marco   Andrea = Cristina   Chiara
(deceased) (1942–)